DOPPELGÄNGER

ALSO BY DAŠA DRNDIĆ
IN ENGLISH TRANSLATION

Trieste (2012)

Leica Format (2015)

Belladonna (2017)

EEG (2019)

Daša Drndić

DOPPELGÄNGER

*Translated from the Croatian
by S. D. Curtis & Celia Hawkesworth*

A NEW DIRECTIONS PAPERBACK ORIGINAL

Originally published by Samizdat B92 in 2002
Published by arrangement with Istros Books, London

This publication is made possible by the Croatian Ministry of Culture

Manufactured in the United States of America
New Directions Books are printed on acid-free paper
First published as a New Directions Paperbook Original (NDP1457) in 2019
(ISBN 978-0-8112-2891-6)

Library of Congress Control Number: 2019942436

2 4 6 8 9 7 5 3 1

New Directions Books are published for James Laughlin
by New Directions Publishing Corporation
80 Eighth Avenue, New York 10011

ARTUR AND ISABELLA

Oh. He shat himself.

An ordinary day, sunny. Soft sunlight, wintry. A view of the railway tracks. A view of the customs house, people in uniform. In the distance, a bit of sea, without any boats. A lot of noise: from the buses, from the people. This is what is called a commotion. Beneath the window—commotion. The panes quiver, the windows of his living room. They're quivering, like jelly, quivering like a small bird. The glass trembles impatiently. He watches. He listens. He's very still while he listens to everything trembling. He places the palm of his hand on the glass. To check what is actually trembling: whether it's a little or a lot, whether it's trembling gently or violently, just the way it trembles—or might it be him that's trembling? He watches what's happening outside, down below. Beneath the window it is lively. His window-frame is peeling, the wood is coarse, unpolished. Women neglect themselves, become unpolished, coarse. Especially their heels. Especially their elbows. Especially their knees. Men less. Less what? They neglect themselves less. They take care of their heels. Take care of their heels? How do they take care of their heels?

There are three trash cans under the window. That's where poverty's gathered together, below his window. Drunken women gather, cats gather. Life gathers down below, beneath his window. HE is above. Watching. All shat up. His penis is withered, all dried up. The panes are loose. The wood is bare and rotten. Between his buttocks—it's slippery. Warm. Stinky. It stinks. Sliding down the leg of his trousers. Down both. He squeezes his buttocks, he walks and squeezes, *à petits pas*. He puts on a diaper. Looks through the window. Here comes darkness. There goes the day.

Diapers. Incontinence, incompetence, incompatibility. He watches gray-haired ladies weeing in their diapers and smiling. They smile tiny smiles and they smile broad smiles. When they give off big smiles, old ladies quiver. Old ladies in aspic. In buses they piss and smile to themselves. In coffee shops, in cake shops, in threes, in fives, sitting at small marble tables jabbering, some are toothless, nattering over cakes, secretly pissing and smiling. Great, happy invention. Diapers. Each one of them is warm between the legs. Just like once upon a time. In their youth. In joyful times. Long ago.

HE looks at his bulge, it's bulging. Like huge artificial genitals. Inside the bulk there squats a tiny willy, his willy, all shriveled. Dangling. Everything is little. Little meals. Little solitude. Solitude—decrepitude. When the rash appears he powders it with talcum, one should do that, yes, and baby cream rubbed in gently. He strokes the rash between his legs, the inside of his thighs, in circles, tenderly, his willy stands up. (He pomades his wee-covered sons on the island of Vis. Little willies.) His hairs have grown thin. He has very little pubic hair. He's no longer hairy. Transparent skin. All shriveled. Bald. That's your portrait.

Look at yourself.

Such silence.

As thick as shit between the buttocks. Dense.

He's got his features, they have remained. They're there. Look.

He's happy.

Everything is so tidy.

SHE steps into the bathtub cautiously because she's old. The tub is full of bubbles, the water is warm. She runs her hand over her flabby skin, she's got a surplus of skin, with her hand she runs over her flaccid stomach, her tits are in the way, her tits are a bother, capillaries break, let them break, ah, she wees in the tub. The water is warm.

SHE has a collection of earplugs. The earplugs lie on the edge of the bathtub, neatly, in a little box. She plucks them out with her index finger and thumb. She takes the wax ones, the tiny round ones, dappled with yellow from frequent use, no, with dark-brown earwax. Yuk. This is my earwax. It's not yuk. It's my insides. That's how she thinks. She kneads the earplugs with her thumb and her forefinger, moulds them, sticks one into her left ear, another into her right ear. Like when they push into your bowels, into your arsehole. Plugs for this, plugs for that. SHE is a carapace. A shell is all that's left.

She leans back in the tub, the edge is cold. She shuts her eyes. She can't hear any noises from outside. Outside there's nothing but a white void. A hole. A white hole with a dot on the right. The dot is a passageway, an entrance to her head. A tight entrance. A narrow entrance, small. Through it her days wriggle out. In her head there is a rumbling, a silent rumble like the rattling of a 4 hp Tomos motor bought on credit for a plastic boat bought on credit thirty years ago, oh, happy days. There's music in her head, her head is full of tunes.

Astrid is a nice name. Astrid is wholesome and fun, Astrid is capable and not very spiteful.

Ingrid is like her, Astrid.

Iris is a nice name. Iris is strange and not very pretty, but she is charming, yes, definitely.

Sarah is pretty and clever. Always lands on her feet. You could call her a loose woman.

Lana is short and bright. She has a wicked tongue. A sharp tongue.

Adriana is stupid.

Isabellas are good and gentle. Isabellas are special beings. Isabellas are sad because there are terrible people in the world. Isabella, that's me.

5

Isabella likes to paint. Isabella loves color. She doesn't like brown. White doesn't exist for her. Isabella has talent. Being an artist for a living was not something to be taken seriously.

Isabella loves acting. Isabella has been acting her whole life. My real self I keep only for myself, thinks Isabella.

Isabella loves photography. She believes that photographs are frozen memories. Isabella never smiles in photos.

Isabella loves running. She runs whenever she is in a bad mood. Running allows her time for thinking. When she runs she has the impression that she clears away her problems. She runs fast. Recently, since she turned seventy-seven, she isn't as fit as she once was because she doesn't have so many problems. That's why she hasn't run recently.

Today Isabella did some drawing. There was a lot of black. The water's getting cold. Isabella adds warm water. She must get out; she's all wrinkled.

The mirror's misted up.

The old woman asks herself, what's that? What kind of distorted image? From now on I'll dream of garden gnomes, from now on I'll dream fairy tales, Isabella decides. Isabella is drying her heels. Her heels are soft and smooth. Isabella is proud of her smooth heels. She never scrapes them yet they're always smooth. The skin of her heels is thin. Fine.

Isabella has never told stories to anyone. Isabella is alone.

HE and SHE will meet.

They don't know it, they don't know they'll meet while they're getting ready to step into the night, into the night of New Year's Eve, bathed and old and dressed up and alone, as they are preparing to walk the streets of this small town, a small town with many bakeries, an ugly small town.

It's New Year's Eve.
It's now they'll meet, now.
He's seventy-nine and his name is Artur.

🗀 FROM POLICE DOSSIERS
SECTOR: SURVEILLANCE OF MILITARY OFFICIALS — MEMBERS
OF THE (FORMER) YUGOSLAV PEOPLE'S ARMY
SUBJECT: ARTUR BIONDI(Ć), RETIRED CAPTAIN OF THE
YUGOSLAV NAVY.
FILE: 29 S-MO II a/01-13-92 (Excerpt)

Artur Biondi(ć), born in Labin, 1921. Extramarital
son of Maristella Biondi(ć) (deceased) and Carlo
Theresin Rankov (deceased). The father of Artur
Biondi(ć), Carlo Theresin Rankov (deceased), was
born in 1900 on the shores of the river Tanaro, as
the extramarital son of Teresa Borsalino, co-owner
of a hat factory in Alessandria, and the Serbian
military officer of the Austro-Hungarian army under
Ranko Matić (deceased).

Artur Biondi — widowed since 1963. Father of two
(legitimate) sons, now adults. Retired captain of
former Yugoslav Navy. Stationed on the island of
Vis until 1975. Citizen of the Republic of Croatia.
Inactive since 1980. Lives alone. Constitution prominently
asthenic. Height — circa 190 cm, weight
— circa 80 kg. Asocial. Suffers from epilepsy.
Diagnosis: grand mal, *epilepsia tarda*. Behavior occasionally
bizarre. Owns a rich collection of hats
and caps. Never leaves his house bareheaded.

7

Artur is wearing a black hat. The brim is broad. Artur is walking behind Isabella. He's looking at Isabella's hair from behind. That's pretty hair, curly. That's black hair. It's swaying. Her hair sways lazily, sleepily. He has no hair. Isabella doesn't know that, she doesn't know his name is Artur and that he has no hair. She'll find out. Artur's walking behind Isabella. He catches up with her. *My name is Artur*, he says. With his right hand Artur touches the brim of his black hat as if he's going to take it off but he's not going to take it off, he just brushes it: that's how it's done. Elegantly. He touches the woman's bent elbow, bent, because she has thrust her hand into her coat pocket, that's why it's bent. His touch is like a fallen snowflake. But there are no snowflakes. There is only the black sky. *Happy New Year, Artur.*

My name is Isabella.

🗁 FROM POLICE DOSSIERS
SECTOR: SURVEILLANCE OF CITIZENS
SUBJECT: ISABELLA FISCHER, MARRIED NAME ROSENZWEIG.
FILE: S-C III/05-17-93 (Excerpt)

Isabella Fischer, born January 29, 1923 in Chemnitz, Germany. She had an elder brother and elder sister (Waller and Christina) both transported in 1941 to the Flossenbürg concentration camp where all trace of them is lost. In 1940 Isabella Fischer, with her mother Sonia Fischer, née Leder, flees to her relatives in Belgrade. Her father, Peter Fischer, co-owner of the shoe factory BATA, remains in Chemnitz. In Belgrade, Isabella Fischer obtains false documents and with her friend of Aryan extraction — Juliana Vukas — leaves for the island of Korčula on April 8, 1941. The mother returns to Chemnitz. In 1943 both of Isabella's parents are transported to Theresienstadt, then to Auschwitz. Isabella Fischer remains with hundreds of other Jewish families on the island of Korčula until September 1943. At the height of attacks on the island, she crosses to Bari by boat. In Bari, Isabella Fischer is taken care of by American soldiers. Isabella Fischer speaks German, Italian, and English. In Bari she meets her future husband, Felix Rosenzweig, co-owner of a chocolate factory in Austria. After the war, she learns through the International Red Cross that 36 members of her close and extended family have been exterminated in the concentration camps of Flossenbürg, Auschwitz, and Theresienstadt. Until her husband's death in 1978 she lives in Salzburg, after which she moves to Croatia. She has no children. By profession a photographer, she opens a photography studio under the name Benjamin Vukas. In 1988 she becomes a citizen of the Socialist Federal Republic of Yugoslavia and sells her shop to the Strechen family. She owns a substantial collection of photographs dating from World War II. Pension insufficient to cover living expenses. Receives a regular annuity from Austria of 4.972 ATS per month. Each monetary transfer is accompanied by a box of chocolates and — quarterly — by a pair of women's seasonal shoes. No relatives.

Applies for Croatian citizenship three times. Application rejected twice. After the intervention of Swiss Government, the request of Isabella Fischer, married name Rosenzweig, is granted on February 1 1993.

My name is Isabella, says Isabella, and then she smiles so that he, Artur, can see her full set of teeth. Artur notices at once that she has her own teeth, and therefore doesn't have dentures, he thinks, running his tongue across his small left dental bridge starting from the back. Isabella smiles, she smiles, he sees that she, Isabella, has her own teeth. How come? Artur wonders. My teeth are nicer than his, thinks Isabella, because they're real. My hair is nicer too. I'm nicer all over. And so, without many words, they stroll along. Artur and Isabella, next to each other, trying to walk in step, because they don't know each other and their rhythms, their walking rhythms, are different, but they are trying discreetly to walk together on this deserted New Year's Eve, when all the festivities have ended, the street festivities. It is four o'clock in the morning, January 1.

Those are your teeth? Artur asks anyway. *Are those your teeth?* he asks nervously, and without waiting for an answer he decides: I'll tell her everything about myself. Almost everything.

They are walking. Along streets empty and littered from the New Year celebrations. Artur says: *I'll tell you everything about myself. We're not children. The night is ethereal.*

You don't need to tell me everything, says Isabella.

Artur says: *I used to work for the Yugoslav Navy. I was stationed on Vis. That's where I met my wife.*

Isabella asks: *Were you a spy?*

Artur thinks: That's a stupid question. He says nothing.

I adore spy stories, says Isabella, and skips like a young girl.

My wife had a heart condition. She was confined to her bed. Alongside the Yugoslav Navy I used to do all the housework. I became very proficient. Today I do all the housework without a problem.

How do you iron? asks Isabella

I have two sons, says Artur. *My wife died*, Artur also says.

How do you cook? asks Isabella. They are still walking. Strolling.

I cook fast and well. I like cooking. Slow down a bit, Miss Isabella. Shorten your stride.

They walk. Artur glances quickly at Isabella, askance, and then at the tips of his shoes. The shoes are old. She glances quickly at him, and a bit at the tips of her shoes. She has pretty shoes, she has pretty shoes, new ones, his are cracked, old.

Isabella says: *Why do you have such big hands? You have unexpectedly big hands.*

He really does have big hands. When he left the Navy, he worked as a salesman for years.

He says: *I really do have big hands. When I left the Navy, I worked as a salesman for years. Listen* says Artur and stops. Artur cannot walk and pronounce serious thoughts simultaneously. The woman sits on a stone step of a stone building, next to a shop window. They are on a promenade. The promenade is crowded with shop windows. The promenade is actually crowded with shop windows, one next to the other. There are illuminated shop windows. Illuminated shop windows flooded with light that spills over the stone promenade, so that the promenade shines. The shop windows are lit because it's New Year's Eve, otherwise the shop windows and stores are mostly dark at night because here poverty reigns.

Dark shop windows. Closed stores. Father's shoe shop is dark. Isabella would like new shoes. New shoes, black patent leather shoes because Isabella is twelve and they're giving a school dance and she has to be pretty for the dance. Father teaches her, for days on and off. Father teaches her to waltz, they practice listening to an old record of The Blue Danube, they spin, Isabella and Father, Isabella in Father's arms, it's safe and warm. Father's store is called BATA. There's a poster hanging in the window of Father's shop, a big poster. The huge poster covers the window. Isabella does not see which shoes she would like to buy. She can't see. The poster hides the shoes. There are no lights. The letters on the poster are black and big. Isabella reads and secretly peeks behind the poster, she searches for black patent leather shoes. For the shoes she'll never buy.

On the 21st day of December 1935, in this shoe shop, Ilse Johanna Uhlmann, typist at AEG, purchased footwear from the Jew Peter Fischer.

On the 23rd day of December 1935, Arno Lutzner, a salesman for AGFA, bought a pair of slippers from the Jew Peter Fischer, co-owner of the BATA store.

On the 29th day of December 1935, Johannes Weichert, Head of the Isolation Ward of Chemnitz Hospital, bought three pairs of shoes.

In compliance with Act 2 of the Decree of Prohibition of the Purchasing of Goods in Jewish Stores, issued September 15, 1935, the above-listed citizens are to report at the local police station by noon of December 30, 1935, at the latest.

Citizens are informed that Jewish stores are under constant surveillance by photographers engaged by the local government. Whoever enters a Jewish shop will be photographed and will suffer all the consequences specified by law.

W. Schmidt, Mayor of Chemnitz

Isabella sits on the yellow bench in the park, opposite her father's BATA shoe shop, singing along to "The Blue Danube." Singing. The bench has been newly painted. The dance is canceled. The dance has been canceled for Jews. The school is closed. The bench is yellow. Isabella doesn't go to school anymore. Isabella goes into her father's shop and sits there, she doesn't want to sit on the yellow bench, she wants to sit among her father's shoes. In the dark shop. In the deserted shop. It is the winter of 1935.

They cut off Doctor Johannes Weichert's beard in the main square. People watch and say nothing. Dr. Johannes Weichert wears a board on his back. Dr. Weichert the sandwich man. On the board it says: *Ich habe von den Juden gekauft.* In big black letters.

Artur watches the woman sitting on the stone threshold of a house on the promenade with shop windows, the woman's name is Isabella, he looks at her from above. He says: *I'm rich but lonely. I have houses, three of them, I have land, I have money. We're grown-ups, there's no sense in equivocating. We could give it a try.*

In what sense? asks Isabella.

Artur slides down next to the woman. Now both are sitting on the stone threshold, gazing in front of them at the littered promenade. There's paper, there are colored ribbons, there is confetti, there are glasses and bottles and tin cans. There are two tall fir trees decorated with paper bows, because baubles get stolen. Isabella and Artur are seated, leaning on a heavy wooden door. Behind the door is a long dark corridor. Behind the door it is dark. They sit leaning against the entrance in the dark. Outside. Sitting on the stone threshold, in the middle of the promenade. Their shoulders touch. Barely. Their legs are bent at the knees.

The woman lays the palm of her hand on Artur's knee, Artur has a bony knee. Isabella's hand drops between Artur's legs. *You wear diapers,* says Isabella. *You wear diapers,* she says, and stretches out her legs. Then she spreads her legs apart; she spreads her outstretched legs apart. *Touch,* she says.

Artur touches. *Diapered ones,* says the woman. *Slide your hand under.*

Under where? asks Artur.

You have a nice hat, says Isabella. *Slide it under the diaper.*

The night is moonless, says Artur and slides his hand under Isabella's skirt, he fumbles, he rummages, he muddles. *This is a strange town,* whispers Isabella, her heart missing a beat, she sighs, ah, and breathes deeply. Isabella sits in her diaper, her legs apart, she sits on the stone threshold and waits. Through the diaper Artur fights his way (somehow) to Isabella's skin. Isabella has a long neck with a tiny Adam's apple sliding up and down as she watches what Artur is doing. Isabella says: *I'll take hold of you too, Mr. Artur. We're adults, there's no point in beating about the bush.* Isabella adds: *This town is full of boredom.*

The old lady is dry. Down there. All dry. *I'm dry,* says Isabella. *Mr. Artur, you have a fat finger.*

Isabella's hand is in Artur's trousers. (Artur moans.) In her palm Isabella holds Artur's small penis, his small, shriveled penis. The diapers are—thank god—dry. Both hers and his are clean and dry. In her closed hand Isabella holds Mr. Artur's penis, she holds his penis and rubs. Up and down.

"A"
Abwehr
down
Adolf
up
Anschluss
down
Appellplatz
up
Arbeit macht frei
down
Aktion
up

Arier Rasse
down
Aktion Erntefest
Aktion Reinhard
Anschluss
up
Auf gut deutsch
Antisemitismus
Auschwitz

Isabella's hand hurts. Isabella slows down.
A bit faster, please, a bit faster, Miss Isabella.

"B"
Blut und Boden
down up down
up down
"E"
Einsatzkommandos
Endlösnung
Eugenik
Euthanasie
"G"
Gestapo
down-n'-up-n'-down-n'-up-n'-down-n'-up-n'-down
Genozid
"H"
Herrenvolk
Häftlingspersonalbogen
"J"
Jude

Judenfrei
Judengelb—yellow, yellow
Juden raus!
Die Juden—unser Unglück
Judenrat
up
Judenrein
up n' down n' up n' down when will he come?
"K"
Kapo
Kommando
KPD—Thälmann
Krematorium
Kriminalpolizei
Kristallnacht Chemnitz
up-and-down
"L"
Lager
Lagersystem
Lebensraum
Lebensunwertes Lebens
Hitler under "H"
we're almost there, up n' down n' down n' down n'
"M"
Mein Kampf
Muselmänner
"O"
Ordnungspolizei
Ostministerium—Rosenberg.
"P"
Pogrom

"R"
Rassismus
"S"
Sonderkommando
"T"
Thanatologie
"U"
Übermenschen
"V"
Vernichtung
down n' up n' down n' up n' down
"Z"
Zyklon B

Done.

A one-minute hand job, ten years of history, ten years of Isabella's life. Isabella's hand is full of Artur's lukewarm diluted sperm.

Isabella has small hands. Artur hasn't got much sperm.

Artur's finger, which finger Isabella asks herself, the middle or the index finger, Mr. Artur has big fingers, his finger finds its way, enters, and inside it twists and turns it turns and goes a bit in and a bit out, in and out and in and out.

You're no longer dry, says the old man, *I've turned you on,* says Artur. *Yes,* says Isabella, *I haven't been turned on for a long time. Now I have to pee.*

And so, on the stone step they sit and gaze straight ahead with glassy eyes, with dead eyes, like fish, no one passes by, they touch like children.

Where do you buy your hats?

I have a rich collection of hats, says Artur. *I have a distant cousin through whom I get my hats,* Artur adds. He says that quietly.

DOCUMENT: A.B./S-P IVc 31-10-97
A DEBRIEFING INTERVIEW BETWEEN THE INVESTIGATOR TITO FRANK (HENCEFORTH REFERRED TO AS "THE INVESTIGATOR") AND THE HATTER, THOMAS WOLF (HENCEFORTH "WOLF") ON 31 OCT. 1997

Investigator: You are a hatter?

Wolf: I am a creator of hats. There is a difference.

Investigator: How long have you been working in this profession?

Wolf: Sixty years. I inherited the store and the workshop from my father.

Investigator: Where was your father from?

Wolf: Lombardy.

Investigator: You also create hats for the president. How did that happen?

Wolf: Excuse me. I created hats for both presidents.

Investigator: What kind of hats were those?

Wolf: Black. The model is called President. They are always called President but they are never the same.

Investigator: You only made hats for the presidents?

Wolf: No. Due to market pressures I had to widen my range.

Investigator: Who are your customers?

Wolf: We are a successful family firm. We have many customers. Ask if the great author Krleža bought from us?

Investigator: Forget Krleža. Who buys your hats nowadays?

Wolf: Krleža was a special customer. He didn't often order in person. He had the use of a car, I think it was an Opel, and his chauffeur would take the hats. We would make the hats according to the rules of the trade, but Krleža would squash them, distort them a bit, and only then put them on his head. Today lots of different people buy our hats. Politicians and ordinary people.

Investigator: How do politicians take to your hats?

Wolf: Obediently. It doesn't occur to them to knead them into shape.

Investigator: Who else?

Wolf: What do you mean who else?

Investigator: Who else buys them?

Wolf: The writer Marija Jurić Zagorka bought them. She had a large circumference: 61 cm. After the Second World War women covered their heads with scarves, they didn't frequent our store.

Investigator: Is it true that you created the first officers' hats?

Wolf: In which period are you referring to? When our business first opened, my father created hats only for women. I am the best hatter in this town. And further.

Investigator: You also provide a dog-training service? For police dogs?

Wolf: In my youth, I was also a boxer. Right now I am a member of the local mountaineering club. I climb the lower heights. Mostly on Sundays.

Investigator: Were you in the war?

Wolf: Which war are you referring to?

Investigator: What is your opinion of our politicians?

Wolf: They are all bigheads. They all have circumferences bigger than 60 cm. My hats have a soul.

Investigator: Do you create hats from your own imagination or do your customers tell you what they're looking for?

Wolf: Some people need advice. Presidents don't like to change models. They stick to one style. Always the same.

Investigator: How often does the president change his hat in a year?

Wolf: The president isn't a big fan of hats. He has maybe four or five hats, and those are the ones we gave him as presents. He didn't buy new ones. Sometimes he sends his hats to be brushed. He keeps them well. Those in his entourage who take care of his wardrobe have a problem: his hats would always get destroyed during travel. That's why we sent him a hat box. Good thing the president doesn't travel often.

Investigator: Does the president pay by card or with cash?

Wolf: The president doesn't pay. We wouldn't allow that.

Investigator: Who else wears your hats?

Wolf: Members of the Senate. Mostly those of the right-wing party. They are the majority.

Investigator: Do you have a favorite head of state?

Wolf: I made a Slavonian hat for Genscher.

Investigator: You once said that big heads were cleverer than small heads.

Wolf: There are always exceptions.

Investigator: Does the making of women's hats differ in any way from the making of men's hats?

Wolf: Women's hats are considerably more pliable. For men's hats you often need physical strength to work the material. Women's hats take more time; they are not made in multiple copies.

Investigator: What opinion do you have of the Croatian people based on their choice of hats?

Wolf: I don't have an opinion.

Investigator: Do you know Artur Bondić?

Wolf: His surname is Biondi. He is the greatest wearer of hats in this country. We are distantly related.

Isabella lifts her left hand (the right hand is still in Artur's trousers), touches his hat, takes the hat off the old man's head, puts it on her own head, puts it back on the old man's, on his hairless head, the old man is called Artur.

Why? Why do you collect hats?

This town has no class, says Artur. *My grandmother was Italian. From Alessandria. Her name was Teresa,* he adds.

Once upon a time, Artur's mother tells him, *once upon a time, Serbian officers in the Austro-Hungarian army were stationed in barracks in Lombardy. Alessandria is in Lombardy,* says his mother. *Serbian officers go out in Alessandria looking for women, because the town is full of pretty girls, yes. Later, the town was full of hats,* says his mother. *I'll tell you a story,* she says.

Once upon a time there was a young man named Giuseppe. In the year 1857 he came to Alessandria, caught a heap of rabbits and started making hats from their fur. The business flourished. When Giuseppe died, he left behind a large hat factory. That was in 1900. His factory made 750,000 hats a year. Many people worked in his factory. Giuseppe had a son and a daughter. The son took over the factory and the daughter's name was Teresa. Years passed by. Hat production increased immensely. The hats were exported to every corner of the world. Two million people walked the globe wearing hats from tiny Alessandria. When Fascism came, production fell and you, Artur, were small, mother tells him. *When Fascism comes there are more important things to produce.*

There is a dish called Escalope Borsalino. It's served in France. Artur has been to France, to the Loire, he visited the castles on an organized tour. That's why he knows.

Alessandria lies on a river. The river is called the Tanaro. It has banks covered with rushes and rushes rustle in the wind, they rustle like whispers.

So Artur reads guidebooks and studies the small history of the Alessandria where his father was born, in the rushes.

See, it's like a fairy tale, Miss Isabella. That Alessandria.

I adore fairy tales.

Artur adores his hats, he doesn't know what he'd do without them, how he'd live without them. His hats are his past. And his present. His sons no longer visit him.

This model is called Borsalino Como.

It's a nice model.

It's made of fur felt, rabbit fur.

It's a hat for conclusive, sorry, exclusive occasions. It's extremely expensive.

How much?

Four hundred and twenty thousand lire.

Isabella quickly takes her hand out of Artur's trousers and wipes it on her thick brown stockings. On her brown stockings opaque white smears appear. *There are no chocolate balls that expensive. No, there aren't,* whispers Isabella. She brings her hand to her nose. Sniffs. *They smell authentic,* she says. Artur nevertheless brings his middle finger to his mouth. Sucks. Artur sucks his middle finger as if he has just cut it.

From her pocket Isabella takes two chocolate balls. The chocolate balls are hard. Compact. You have to hold them in your palms for a long time before they become soft. It's cold outside. Isabella adores chocolate balls. There are lots of different ones on offer, different makes for sale. Isabella is a real connoisseur. Isabella knows chocolate balls filled with pieces of candied orange or raspberry: orangeade and Razzmatazz balls, perfect balls, perfect for mornings that follow bad dreams. Isabella knows the dark, bitter balls Choc-a-lot and Loca Moca, she saves them for when she watches thrillers on television because they are exciting and keep her mind alert. Isabella eats milk chocolate balls when she feels loneliness coming on. She saves the milk chocolate balls to comfort her in different ways; mostly for small troubles, daily ones. She throws them into her mouth and rolls them left and right with her tongue, gently. Then, when they have melted to the right texture, exactly right, Isabella penetrates them with a sharp movement of her tongue, enters inside them, breaks in. With her tongue. Inside, in her chocolate balls, a different sweetness is waiting. Soft cream, thick cream, across her palate, across her mouth cavity, it spreads out like tiny kisses, like a velvet cloak. Then Isabella closes her eyes and smacks her lips. Her Carmelita, her Nutropolis, her Coco Motion and Butterscotch-cha-cha. Her music, yes, oh yes. Lindor chocolate balls, packed in boxes of 48 for 50 marks—one ball, one mark. Lindor chocolate balls are eaten deliberately. Isabella eats them sparingly. Ferrero Rocher come in smaller boxes of only 30 balls. Baci Perugina are crunchy inside, like the bites of her nervous lover. Most of all Isabella likes Swiss Teuscher balls, she knows them best, she knows them inside out, thoroughly. Marzipan, fruit, all kinds of fruit, walnuts, almonds, hazelnuts, dark chocolate, white chocolate, milk chocolate, raisins, coffee, all kinds of joy from the imagination of Dolf Teuscher, in his village in the Swiss Alps. A hundred and one chocolate secrets hidden in the chocolate balls of Dolf Teuscher. Dolf Teuscher, the great lover. Rum balls, coconut balls, balls filled with Irish coffee and balls filled with maraschino in which floats a tiny cherry. Yes! Chocolate balls with tiny inebriated cherries, all spaced out, dark red like a drop of Isabella's blood, like her clitoris in the days of her youth. My little cherry, that's what Isabella calls her clitoris. Her clitoris is no longer red, it doesn't pulsate, it's not soaked with passion. Her clitoris is slack and pale pink. *I've got an anaemic clitoris,* says Isabella. Artur helps himself to a chocolate ball. *Here's an almond inside,* says Isabella, *not a cherry.*

Artur munches. The chocolate sticks to Artur's palate. The softened chocolate, blending with Artur's saliva, runs slowly down Artur's front teeth. Artur smiles. He has a brown smile, a little brown smile because he is clenching his teeth, because the chocolate ball isn't very sweet. *It's bitter*, says Artur, and keeps on smiling. Artur looks foolish. It's now four o'clock and forty-five minutes. The dawn still hasn't arrived. It's cold.

That's a new one, says Isabella.

The new chocolate was launched in Chemnitz. From 1953 to 1990, Chemnitz was called Karl-Marx-Stadt. The balls are wrapped in red tinfoil with a picture of Karl Marx on them. The balls carry Karl Marx's portrait printed on them, all in chocolate, including the beard. In Chemnitz, long ago, they erected a bust of Karl Marx. The sculpture was placed in the center of town. That's logical, it's logical that Karl Marx's bust be installed in the center of a former East German town previously called Karl-Marx-Stadt. The bust weighs 42 tons. Karl Marx wrote the Communist Manifesto.

Isabella agrees: the chocolate balls with Karl Marx on them are not very tasty. The silver paper is pretty. It has a star. It can be used for wrapping up walnuts and hanging on Christmas trees. Like in her childhood, her youth. Isabella knows Chemnitz.

Isabella is thirteen. The headmaster of her school removes the statues of two boys, the statues are on top of the building. They are there as decoration. There are eight of them, eight statues, the headmaster takes two of them away. The headmaster orders that the statues be destroyed. Grown-ups smash the statues, they smash the statues of the two boys. Downstairs, in front of the school, with stone hammers, they violently smash the boys to pieces. Isabella watches. The blows echo. Children watch. The boy Moritz was the sculptor's model, Isabella doesn't know the name of the sculptor, he's no longer in Chemnitz. Moritz is a Jew. The boy Moritz is a Jewish boy and his likeness must be destroyed.

People are leaving Chemnitz. Mama says, *Let's go,* Daddy says, *I'll watch the store.* People leave. The invisible leave. Daddy says, *We won't go. We won't go yet.* After the war, people return to Chemnitz. Fifty-seven people return. After the war. Chemnitz is a small place. A small number of people return. Now a new century is beginning. A new return to Chemnitz. Chemnitz has three hundred Jews. Chemnitz gets a new synagogue. People set the old synagogue alight; Isabella Fischer's neighbors burn down the old synagogue. The flames are high, the night is cold, it's November of 1938, it's the eighth of November 1938, fires everywhere. Isabella watches. Isabella is fifteen years old, she's no longer small.

Chemnitz has become a part of Flossenbürg. A part of the camp of Flossenburg. Chemnitz has become a concentration camp, but a tiny one.

Isabella always unwraps her chocolate balls with care so that she can save the silver paper. Over the year, she collects the foil wrappers in a book beside her bed because she eats most of the chocolate balls in bed. When she finishes the book, she will put the wrappers into another one. At the moment she's reading an exciting book. The book is called This Way for the Gas, Ladies and Gentlemen. She puts the Karl Marx foil wrappers in it. By the end of the year, she will have collected a lot of wrappers for the Christmas tree, more for the branches she hangs on the walls because trees are expensive, branches can be found amongst the waste, in the trash, one could say, in the trash. But Isabella doesn't wrap up walnuts anymore. She sorts out the shiny ones. There are different sorts. Blue with silver stars, or silver with blue stars, Isabella can't remember at the moment, but nevertheless, they are like little skies, like little skies you can put in your pocket. Isabella has many little square heavens (Baci Perugina) inside the book she is reading: This Way for the Gas, Ladies and Gentlemen. In her youth, space was enormous, the night sky filled with silver dust that seemed infinite and close enough to touch. Now it is small and here, she can touch it, stroke it, put it in her pocket, put it in a book. Isabella doesn't know why she is reading that particular book, this book that is amusingly called This Way for the Gas, Ladies and Gentlemen. There are more amusing books, there are better books. Isabella knows that. She reads all kinds of books. *Why should I read him, that Borowski?*

Why do I stick to Borowski?

🗁 FROM POLICE DOSSIERS
SECTOR: SURVEILLANCE OF CITIZENS
SUBJECT: ISABELLA FISCHER, MARRIED NAME ROSENZWEIG.
NUMBER: P-G III/12-19-99 (Excerpt)

Bought with her monthly allowance for December 1999, Isabella Fischer, married name Rosenzweig, received a book by the controversial communist spy and propagandist Tadeusz Borowski, born in the Ukraine to parents of Polish origin. In spite of the fact that the book speaks of Borowski's experience in the camps of Auschwitz and Dachau, which he somehow managed to survive, the arrival of other books by Borowski may be expected — books that promote communist ideology and philosophy.

The fact that Borowski is not alive does not diminish the power of his words. On the contrary.

Borowski, born in 1922, committed suicide by gas poisoning in his flat in 1951.

Maybe Isabella is looking for something, some answer, some clue, some glimmer. Maybe Borowski knew Waller and Christine, maybe he met Mama Sonya and Daddy Peter, there. And? When she's read This Way for the Gas, Ladies and Gentlemen, she will read other books, surely, yes. She will read lighter books, warmer. She will read about garden gnomes. They are more appropriate for the collecting of shiny, rustling wrappers with the scent of chocolate.

Save the wrappers, Isabella says.

Isabella carefully opens her Karl Marx ball and smooths the foil across her knee with the outside edge of the thumb of her right hand.

I used to have a dog, says Artur.

I have garden gnomes, says Isabella. Then adds: *They don't die.*

Artur doesn't see well. Artur doesn't know if he ate the chocolate Marx. He's hungry. He's cold. He can still taste the chocolate bitterness.

When Chemnitz was called Karl-Marx-Stadt the inhabitants didn't ask for the 42-ton Marx, it came by itself. Now they don't know what to do with it. They hope that the town will become famous for the chocolate balls.

Artur has been to Salszburg. They have Mozart balls there, with marzipan inside. They are delicious. He hasn't been to Chemnitz, nor to Karl-Marx-Stadt. These balls are not worth a piece of shit. *Here's your silver paper,* says Artur.

I've got more, says Isabella, *try this one.* She offers Artur a Strauss cube, actually a Droste praline. *It's a cube,* says Isabella, *not a ball.* Isabella carefully opens her Strauss cube and almost to herself she adds: *These cubes are expensive, but your hat is more expensive. These are Strauss cubes. A large box costs two hundred and forty marks. I prefer Tchaikovsky. His music relaxes me the way Mozart balls do. Tchaikovsky hasn't got chocolate balls named after him.*

Tchaikovsky was an epileptic, says Artur. *So was Handel.*

Alfred Nobel was an epileptic too, says Isabella. *And Thomas Edison. And Paul the Apostle.*

Artur is shaking. Artur is afraid he'll have an epileptic fit. Artur is an epileptic. When he has an attack, he fills his diaper. When he gets an attack he is filled with a joyous feeling, he floats, he hears music, and the music whispers to him, secrets which are otherwise beyond his grasp. His epilepsy is his friend, it is his companion, his small invisible secret love that tortures him and bestows gifts. Well, without his fits, without his seizures, convulsions, jerking, without his petit mal, his falling-down disease, his sacred disease, he would be completely alone. But at this moment Miss Isabella is here, and they are eating Strauss cubes that are so much better than Karl Marx balls, and they are enjoying themselves. Artur implores his lover to postpone her visit. Byron, Edward Lear, Dostoevsky, Flaubert, Dickens, Agatha Christie, Truman Capote. Artur studies famous epileptics. Mark Twain. Napoleon. Alexander the Great, Julius Caesar. Peter the Great, Socrates, Pythagoras, Van Gogh, da Vinci, Michelangelo.

History is full of epileptics. That's nothing to worry about, says Isabella.

It seems that Artur and Isabella complement each other.

We complement each other, says Artur.

I cannot complement anybody, says Isabella. *I'm empty.*

Isabella's flat is full of gnomes. Isabella lives in a flat. She doesn't have a garden. You can't call her gnomes garden gnomes. They are home gnomes. Two white ones are placed at the front entrance, greeting her when she comes home. She always comes home. They have tall hats. Isabella's flat seems spacious, open, like a garden. It has no doors. It has no internal walls. Isabella had all the walls knocked down. Isabella tells the white gnomes her life story. They are silent and listen. Sometimes, Isabella touches them. The gnomes have their leader. The gnomes keep her safe from earthquakes. Isabella loves fairy tales. If she had a garden, Isabella would have it full of winding paths and gnomes. Crisscrossing paths that would confuse evil spirits. Isabella wants to go home.

🗁 FROM POLICE DOSSIERS
SEARCH OF FLAT BY ORDER OF CHIEF OF CITY POLICE ON JANUARY 1ST 2000 FROM 4:07 TO 5:02 A.M. REPORT. SUBJECT: ISABELLA FISCHER, MARRIED NAME ROSENZWEIG. NO: 38 S-C I/01-01-00 (EXCERPT)

✔ The flat is tidy and spacious. The only separate room is a bathroom (with toilet). No internal walls. The whole flat is some 70 m2.

✔ 36 garden gnomes arranged throughout the flat. Some are completely white, others have their clothes painted red, yellow, green, blue. Some of the gnomes are smiling. There are male and female gnomes. Some of them are exceptionally short, some tall, almost large. Every gnome has a metal ID plate hanging round its neck. In compliance with previously collected data, it may be concluded that those are the names of the deceased members of Isabella Rosenzweig's (née Fischer) family.

✔ Throughout the living space, on the floor and on the furniture, lie boxes of chocolates. A count of 77 boxes. There are boxes of different shapes and sizes, of world-famous brands. The chocolate boxes carry the labels of: Manner, Lindt, Droste, Suchard, Nestlé, Milka, Neuhaus, Cardullos, La Patisserie, Asbach/Reber, Biffar (the only box of candied fruit, the rest contain chocolate), Hacher, Underberg. Some of the sweets have unusual names. A conspicuously large number of chocolate balls bear the inscription "Joy of Life" and "Karl Marx Kugeln." ALL THE BOXES HAVE BEEN OPENED.

✔ The price labels on the boxes are proof of their quality. The prices range from 40 to 60 DEMs per box. The Strauss are the most expensive chocolates, actually praline cubes, which cost 180 DEM. In the box there is also a CD. Supposedly with the music of Strauss. On the floor are large tin boxes on which the names "Constance and Amadeus" are written. Chocolate Constance and Amadeus balls are made by the company Reber.

✔ A number of silver squares were found by the bed,

wrappers from the aforementioned chocolate balls. A book with an English title: This Way for the Gas, Ladies and Gentlemen. The author is a certain Tadeusz Borowski.

✔ A number of adult diapers were found in the bathroom. The bath was unwashed and damp. On the edge of the bathtub, a small box containing 6 pairs of earplugs, of varying shape and material.

✔ The kitchen area in disorder. Fridge: 4 boxes of Kraš chocolates, a dried head of garlic, 2 eggs and some withered vegetables. The other shelf space is taken up with unwashed dishes.

✔ At the entrance, ten pairs of women's shoes. All in excellent condition. Of obvious quality.

✔ Search ended at 5:02 a.m. due to notification that tenant was on her way home.

Artur wants to go home too.

🗁 FROM POLICE DOSSIERS
SEARCH OF FLAT BY ORDER OF CHIEF OF CITY POLICE ON JANUARY 1ST 2000 FROM 3:45 TO 5:10 A.M.
REPORT. SUBJECT: ARTUR BIONDI(Ć), RETIRED CAPTAIN OF YUGOSLAV NAVY.
No: 37 S-MO I/ 01-01-00 /(Excerpt).

✔ The flat is tidy. The shelves are mostly taken up with books on epilepsy, hats, and Italy.

✔ In the bathroom — a large quantity of disposable diapers for adults. Bathroom — clean

- ✔ Kitchen — modern and stylish. Fridge stuffed with food. There are expensive delicacies, some in jars (caviar and marinated herring)
- ✔ A larger room has been adapted into a walk-in wardrobe:
- ✔ Suits: 17 (old-fashioned)
- ✔ Shoes: 10 pairs (worn-out)
- ✔ Shirts: 36 pieces, various styles. All made of natural materials: cotton, batiste, satin and silk. Threadbare.
- ✔ Hats and caps: the left sidewall — 3.75 m in height and 5.5 m in width — from top to bottom covered with shelves. On the shelves, hats and caps arranged by manufacturer's brand and by name of article. All items in perfect condition.
- ✔ Noticeable high quality of all apparel, especially the hats. On some of the headwear a price is still visible. The room is reminiscent of a miniature museum. On some articles there is a short informative text. For example (a text taken from the photograph): *BERET: Appeared first in France at the beginning of the 19th century. Mostly worn by French peasants and herdsmen in the Basque country. Later the beret was taken up by artists and bohemians, as a symbol of protest against the prevailing social system. Also worn by members of the French Resistance during the Second World War. The modern army wears them for everyday usage. Che Guevara also contributed to their popularity. In the 1990s the beret is still a favorite with men and women alike.*

Shelf contents:

- ✔ Woollen berets, diameter 28 cm, ordinary. Make no longer visible: blue, black, brown, dark red, green. Price: 18.000 LIT per item (11 items).
- ✔ A special place is reserved for Borsalino berets. Description: *Borsalino berets are made by one of the most renowned manufacturers of headwear. They are made of pure lambswool, lined with satin. Sizes range from: 55, 57, 61 and for particularly large heads — 63 cm. Price: 70.000 LIT apiece.* Sizes present: 59 and 61 cm. Colors: black, gray, dark blue (7 pieces).
- ✔ 1 Hoquy beret. Description: *manufactured in the family-run workshop of Hoquy, a competitor of Borsalino. Has produced headwear for over two hundred years. The workshop is located near the Pyrenees. Price: 90.000 LIT apiece.* Shelf contents: 5 pieces — 2 black, 1 gray and two blue.
- ✔ Anglo-Basque beret made by Kangol. 100% wool. 3 pieces. Price: 58.000 LIT
- ✔ Parkhurst beret: *cotton. Worn by men and women. Manufactured in one standard size.* Price: 24.000 LIT. 5: 2 wine-red, 1 red, 1 beige, 1 olive green.
- ✔ Bankroft army beret, so-called Green Beret. *Manufacturer: the same name as the American firm that supplies the US Army. Made famous by General Montgomery in the battle for El Alamein.*
- ✔ Six identical pieces.
- ✔ Drover hats. Description: *can withstand rain, wind and sun. Price: 71.000 LIT.* 2 pieces (1 beige and 1 brown).

✔ Hats of different makes: Henschel Aussie, Kangol, Biltmore (150.000 LIT), Akubra (230.000 LIT), soft felt fedora hats made by Christy's, Stacy Adams, Stetson Saxon, Rosellini and Borsalino — these take up 6 shelves. Their prices range from 196.000 to 368.000 LIT.

✔ Below are a dozen Homburg models, mostly black. Prices from 220.000 to 360.000 LIT.

✔ Artur Biondi(ć) owns fifteen Panama hats, all famous brands. The most expensive piece is Montecristi Superfino from the Equatorial province of Manabí. Biondi(ć) states that the hat is handmade out of palm-fiber cloth: paja toquilla — Carloduvica palmata. Price — 570.000 LIT (2 pieces). Biondi(ć) also has one of the cheaper models of the Panama hat — Montecristi Fino (290,000 LIT). All three hats are in natural colors (from label).

✔ On the shelf, next to the Montecristi hat, a small plastic box with a stand, is a framed computer printout of "Legends of the Panama hat." No computer or printer was found in the flat. The legend reads: *Upon arrival in the New Country, the first settlers, Spaniards, saw that some natives were wearing strange head coverings. Their caps were made of light, transparent material. The immigrants believed that it was the skin of skinned vampires. But in archaeological excavations on the Equator Coast, ceramic figures with the unusual caps on their heads were found, supposedly dating from the year 4,000 BC. These are the first variants of today's Panama hat.*

✔ Stetsons — 3 pieces, black. One with a 9.5 cm brim and a crown height of 10 cm, and two larger (brim — 10 cm, crown — 12 cm) All three hats are set in silver satin (from label). Price 300.000 LIT a piece.

✔ Straw hats — 8, various models. Short history attached.

✔ Bowler hats — 4. White Nürnberg (155,000 LIT), Homburg olive green (139,000 LIT), black Borsalino (430,000 LIT) and a Piccadilly from 1936 produced at Jakša Žuljević's workshop in Split — no price.

✔ Top hats — 2. One black (460.000 LIT) and one gray (370.000 LIT), both of satin. According to the labels, the black one is foldable, the gray one is indivisible. Below is a short text on the fate of the top hat through history, taken from the Encyclopedia of the Yugoslav Lexicographic Institute, year of issue 1967.

✔ On one shelf there is a collection of decorative pins. As a distinctive female hat decoration, it does not fit into Arturo Biondi(ć)'s men's collection. There are 23 pieces. They are housed in glass boxes on black plush. Some are very old and obviously have antique value. Each pin has a description and place of origin. There are no prices. Attached is a short history of decorative pins (for hats) from the late nineteenth to late twentieth century.

✔ In addition to decorative pins, there is another item that does not fit in the hat and headwear collection described above: a miniature women's hat labelled "Doll's Hat." Under the description

is the text: *First issued in 1938. A miniature doll's hat, slightly crooked, worn by adult
women on the front right-hand side of the head.
As soon as it appeared, it caused numerous con-
troversies. Two years later it disappeared from
the market and from use. The doll's hat was
mostly green or purple and adorned by a large
Emu feather. Undocumented observers would now
conclude that women of that age had miniature
heads, of course, which could only accommodate a
miniature brain.* (Text downloaded with enlarged
photos.)

✔ Found: a total of 274 hats and caps.
✔ Photos enclosed.
✔ Search ended at 5:30 a.m. due to notification
  that Artur Biondi was approaching the building.

Look at yourself.

Such silence.

Thick as shit between the buttocks. Thick.

You have features. They're here.

Look at yourself in the window. The window is black. Behind it
lies the night. Look how clear your image in the window is.

On the surface of the water float flakes of Isabella's dead skin. Isabella is being flayed. She can't say why her skin is dying. She's got
too much skin. Today Isabella did some drawings. There was a lot
of black. The water's getting cold. Isabella adds some warm water.
She must get out, she'll shrivel. Isabellas are good and gentle. Isabellas are special beings.

The Daily News

Sunday, January 2, 2000.

Woman Hangs Herself in Attic of Block of Flats

Isabella F. (77) committed suicide by hanging.

According to the information obtained from the local police, the unfortunate elderly woman died in the early morning hours of Saturday, January 1. The body of the woman was found hanging in the attic of the building where she lived. The possible reason that led Isabella F. to perform such an act so far remains unknown. Following their examination of the place of suicide the local police released information to the press.   (D.R.)

Man Kills Himself by Jumping from Window

Artur B. (79) committed suicide on Saturday, January 1 by jumping from his living room window.

According to information given out at a press conference called by the police, the elderly man committed suicide between 5:30 and 6:30 a.m. on the first day of the New Year. So far, any motive that could have led Artur B. to perform such an act remains unknown. The police have no information about whether the old man suffered from any serious illness that could have driven him to suicide. The investigation at the scene of the incident was carried out by the Criminal Officers of the City Police Administration.   (B.O.)

📁 FROM POLICE DOSSIERS
SUBJECT: ARTUR BIONDI(Ć), RETIRED CAPTAIN OF THE
YUGOSLAV NAVY.
NUMBER: 39 D-C Ia /01-02-00

Artur Biondi(ć) committed suicide on January 1,
2000, by jumping from his living room window on the
seventh floor. He was found lying motionless by the
trash cans (three of them) in front of the building he lives (lived) in. The autopsy confirmed that
death had occurred immediately after the fall. Time
of death: between 5:30 and 6:30 a.m.

    Case "Artur Biondi(ć)" filed *ad acta*.

📁 FROM POLICE DOSSIERS
SUBJECT: ISABELLA FISCHER, MARRIED ROSENZWEIG.
NUMBER: 40 D-C Ib/01-02-00
Isabella Rosenzweig née Fischer hanged herself in
the attic of the house she lived in. Time of death:
between 5:30 and 6:30 a.m. on January 1, 2000. She
left no letter or message.

    Case "Isabella Fischer married name Rosenzweig"
filed *ad acta*.

Is that a forest? It is wide and spacious. There are trees and there
are no trees. Where there are trees, the trees are small. Where
there are trees, they are puny and short. Maybe it's a magic forest.

Through that space, through that unbounded space resembling a terrestrial cosmos they run, they soar and they lose their way because there's no end. It is impossible to arrive, there is no place to come to. They are seeds, they are grain and they scatter. On a tiny tree a harpy squats and watches. With folded wings it crouches and watches. And picks at leaves. Its belly is covered with feathers. *That's my face,* says Isabella. *That's my face,* says Artur. The branch breaks, it's a tiny branch, a thin branch. The small tree turns red and begins to flow. They are leaves. *We are leaves,* they say. They pluck at themselves and they hang and they touch the ground and they flow. *We pluck at ourselves,* say Isabella and Artur. They have huge eyes, huge eyes like cows', brown and round like Mozart balls. In which there is nothing. No marzipan, no almonds, no crimson cherries. There is only the round dark shell, empty. They do not know, because they are old and forgetful, they do not know that inside them crouch their doppelgängers who whisper, while they piss themselves, while they breathe, slowly and spasmodically, while they tremble, while they eat chocolates. Their disguised doppelgängers threaten and summon them, call out and shout, *come on—join us.*

PUPI

It is drizzling but he cannot move.

I can't move.

Small, fateful, pasts grow in his head. They get mixed up with the drizzle, which is the present.

Most of the rhinos in the world are black. There are gray ones and white ones as well, the white ones are rare. There are fewer and fewer rhinos. They are an endangered species, there are more and more endangered species, that is why there are ever fewer of them. They are disappearing.

He is disappearing too.

I'm disappearing, says Printz. His name is Printz.

Rhinos take on the color of their surroundings. They blend. In cities, their surroundings are gray.

I'm blending, says Printz. *I'm in the city and I'm blending. I'm standing in the zoo watching the rhinos. Everyone can see that. There's no one here. I'm alone. My name is Printz.*

He is in the city, Printz is.

He is in the zoo, watching the rhinos. They are big animals, fat and rough-skinned.

People think they are dangerous animals, ugly animals, but they aren't. Rhinos are no danger to people. I'm no danger to people. Rhinos can be a danger to each other, not to people. They can be a danger to themselves because they destroy each other, destroy themselves. Rhinos are tame and self-destructive. Rhinos aren't bloodthirsty. They're wild beasts, heavy beasts. I'm no longer heavy, I've shrunk. I was handsome, oh, how handsome I was. And big.

Rhinos run at a slow trot, when they run. When they run, they wobble. Their great bodies sway from side to side in slow motion, they sway. Look at them swaying!

Rhinos are like big waves so that scares you, I'm not frightened. The rhinos down there below me are very big. That's all.

Printz stands on a ridge, looking at the two rhinos down below, in their enclosure. It is late autumn. The colors are autumnal, dreary.

I'm watching the rhinos. They're big.

Printz would like to tell someone something, there is no one.

I would like to tell someone, anyone, I'd like to tell someone: I buried Mother today. Mother is called Ernestina, we called her Tina, there's no one around.

Shout. Shout to the rhinos down below, they are down there, in the hollow.

Zoos are not a good place for outings when it's late autumn and cold and you're burying your mother. I feel alone.

He is not alone. He has a father.

My father is old and sad. I'll take him on a trip.

And he has a brother.

My brother's no good now. I'll take my father a long way away.

But no, Printz is not yet alone. Printz's dense solitude is just coming into being. Behind it there is darkness.

My solitude is budding, says Printz. *I feel my solitude budding, I can see my solitude budding, that's why I take deep breaths.*

Printz takes deep breaths on the ridge, watching the rhinos while his solitude swells.

This is like an enormous tomb, where the rhinos live, mother doesn't have a tomb.

The funeral was enough to freeze your feet.

The crematorium is behind muddy fields because it is new and unfinished. But the furnaces are all right, they work. The furnaces work perfectly. The cemetery is behind the crematory. It is an old cemetery, orderly. It is the third crematorium in the city. It is a big city.

The hall is like a mausoleum, a church, the ceilings are high and painted, it is cold inside. When the music stops playing the coffin disappears and the people look up at the painted ceiling because they feel uncomfortable. Down below are the ovens. Here they do not let the fire lick a glass cabinet in front of everyone, as there are no glass cabinets here. Where the fire burns, in the glass cabinets, the corpses lie in open coffins like jewels in expensive boxes.

In America, they light a fire that fizzles. It's a gas fire, that's why it fizzles. I've seen it.

Printz had been in America, working.

The flame blazes, blazes, blazes, soft music is played (by request), the deceased person bends at the waist, slowly rises, rises, rises and sits, nicely made-up. Deceased American people have nice hairdos and cardboard shoes. So, the American deceased people sit in their nice new coffin until it twists like a burned-out match. They sit in a fine interior of white, pink or red satin. If it is a man, he sits in satin as blue as the sea or sky. That is the way it is from birth. Recently yellow has been introduced, for the sake of equality. Now deceased people glow gold, as though bathed in sunshine. That looks dazzling. Biblical.

What about the eyes of American deceased people? Do the eyes of American deceased people watch? Do they see the beauty of their own departure?

There are no data about the eyes.

Here there is no transparency. There is no watching. Mother is nailed in. The coffin is cheap. There is music, someone makes a speech, Mother disappears, Mother burns but no one sees. Mother is ash.

The urn stays in the depot for five years.

That comes later. Father is still alive.

The depot is large like a warehouse, with white tiles for the sake of hygiene. A store of urns, a store of the dead. Here, within reach.

That comes later. In this city there are two rhinos.

This city used to be handsome, it is not now. It has grown old. It has let itself go. It has been let go, allowed to fall to rack and ruin.

I was handsome once as well. I've let myself go, I'm ruined.

Printz was handsome, he still is, he has let himself go a little. He has not yet been ruined. He will be ruined later on. He will be allowed to be ruined. He will let himself go. Fall to rack and ruin.

The city is now a city with a lot of unfamiliar people in it, earlier it was a city with a lot of familiar people. For the last five years unfamiliar people have been coming in from small towns and they wander about. The familiar people have on the whole died out, some have gone to bigger, more important cities, far away. There is rubbish in this city. The streets have potholes. The trees in the parks have shrunk. Shriveled.

It's got knobbly, like Maristella's knee when she was little.

There used to be a lot of parks, now they are botched, messed-up. Short. Like parks in picture books—they fit into a small space. There used to be huge parks, they stretched in length and breadth all the way to the river, to the confluence of two big rivers there, beneath the fortress. The fortress is old, its name, Kalemegdan, means "great battle," it is a monument to the history of this city. In the park with the fortress there are gates, there are fountains, there are towers, all from the distant past, and from the more recent past, there are busts of folk heroes, a military museum and a small museum with stuffed animals, in front of which a large bear stands, also made by a taxidermist. Near the museum with the stuffed animals, in precisely that park, precisely under the walls of the fortress, there is a zoo with abandoned animals, for such are the times. The biggest monument in the park is called the Monument to the Victor, which, after the recent wars in the former

Yugoslavia sounds terrifying and wrong. Printz used to stand on the ramparts of the fortress watching the rivers merge.

The confluence is murky and muddy now.

From the park you used to see sandy islands in the distance, white islands, now dark with the excrement of pigeons and river gulls.

Gulls eat trash and their shit is black.

In some parks there were trees with hanging branches, so that those parks looked like hanging gardens. There were hiding places. There was soft grass for couples in love. That was in his youth.

That was when Printz was young. I'm Printz.

Printz leaves the rise in the zoo. He goes in search of a hiding place.

The grass is wet and dirty, the grass in the park, the park is big and empty. It is still drizzling. Printz has expensive shoes.

Florsheim shoes, black, with perforations.

In those hiding places dead rats lie, stray dogs whelp, and stray cats have their young there too, there are a lot of strays in this city. In those hiding places animals and people store their inner waste, their intestinal waste, so those hiding places are messy and smelly.

I know, I tour them.

Printz comes to a hiding place behind the northern wall of the fortress. He bends down, peers in, scatters the rubbish with his foot, there are heaps of rubbish: condoms, plastic bags, bloody pads, shit-smeared pieces of toilet paper, sooty candles, crumpled matchboxes, small coins, old coins from his childhood.

I see the coins that fall out of lovers' pockets (mine too, mine too, long ago), lovers rock up and down on the soft grass, the grass used to be soft, they rock on the clean grass, now it's neglected.

Printz is not looking for anything.

I'm not looking for anything. I'm remembering.

He shifts stuff with his foot and listens. Printz feels that soft grass on his back and moves his shoulders as though his Mackintosh was heavy.

It's not a Mackintosh. It's a Burberry. It's drizzling.

Printz raises and drops his shoulders, up and down. Bent over the entrance, examining the hiding place.

This is where I fucked.

Printz raises and drops his shoulders, as though he was saying I don't know. Raises and drops his shoulders, one-two, he feels the grass,

the grass climbs up my back, right up to my throat, up to my throat.

Cry, Printz.

No. The Burberry is heavy, it shouldn't be heavy.

Printz goes back to the zoo.

I'm going back to the zoo. I hear a loud noise.

Printz is standing above the hollow again, above the arena, above the enclosure with the two rhinos in the empty zoo. Printz has wide-open eyes, he looks, he is alone.

It is getting dark.

The city is dark too. A stony half-darkness engulfs it. Indelible. That half-darkness penetrates, ominously. The rhinos are okay.

They're not okay. Something horrible is happening.

In zoos, rhinos are placed in a kind of arena. The arenas are down below, while the visitors are high above them, so that the visitors look at the rhinos from above and do not see details. On one side of the enclosure down below there is an iron door.

A big iron door for rhinos, rhinos are big.

The keepers open that door at night and let the rhinos in, into their little den, their cramped den, their home. The iron door is closed. Bolted.

There are no keepers. The rhinos want to go inside.

The rhinos are restless. They want to go inside.

The rhinos charge. First one, then the other. First the female, then the male. They charge and then, at top speed, their trot becoming a gallop, at a fast gallop, with great force they crash into the iron door, frontally, with their foreheads. They crash into it once, then again. Then they move away, slowly.

It's exhausting.

They reach the other side of the arena and then again, at a gallop—crash head on into the iron door. There is no one around. Only Printz is watching.

Again. Again. Again. Again. Again. Harder. Even harder. Ever harder. The rhinos beat their heads against the iron door while the rain keeps spattering. The earth in the arena is liquid, muddy. The female's horn is dangling, hanging. The male's forehead is bloody.

Under their thick hide there is blood, thick blood, rhino blood.

A new charge. Their horns have burst into bloom like that magician's trick when roses burst open. It gushes from their horns, the redness pours into the rhinos' eyes. Pours. The rhinos are blinded. Maddened.

I don't know much about rhinos, maybe that's a good thing.

The rhinos are dancing. They dance, but their eyes are closed. Blinded with thick blood. They have a curtain, a small red curtain over their eyes and they dance as though listening to music. As though there was music playing all around them. A big dance, like a horses' dance, like a circus dance, but heavy, rhinos are heavy animals.

Do rhinos have eyelashes? Eyelashes collect tears to stop them flowing. My eyelashes are short.

Blinded, the rhinos rise up and fall, they become big black waves, very sluggish. There are a lot of stains on the iron door. Their blows resound like a train in a tunnel, birds fly away.

What a deep rumble!

The rhinos have grasping lips. Their lips are split. They hang.

They do not grasp anything, they cannot grasp anything, and there is nothing anyway. They lick their blood with their tongues.

Do rhinos have tongues?

Rhinos have a lot of blood, the blood is gushing. Both rhinos are lying on their sides like two dark mountains, like two bare hillsides, burned, black, they lie on their sides, in the mud.

They're moving! The living mountains twitch as though they were breathing, falling asleep.

No. The rhinos are not sleeping.

They're shivering.

Now they are breathing steadily, Printz's collar is wet. Printz is shivering. From the rain.

They're licking each other.

Yes. The rhinos' pain is now less. They are licking each other's blood with their dangling grasping lips,

their lips are hanging, limp.

With their split lips hanging on threads of thick rhino hide, they lick each other, tenderly.

Can there be sorrow in rhinos' eyes, I seem to see sorrow in their eyes.

Printz has wide-open eyes. He concentrates hard on the rhinos' breathing down below.

Up above is the heavy sky. Printz does not blink. In the corners of his eyes small drops of fluid gather—round and transparent, and stay there. In the corners of his eyes. As though they were stuck there, as though they were not heavy enough to fall. The small drops in Printz's eyes stay there, shining. Printz does not blink.

Rain has gathered in my eyes, says Printz.

Rhinos are mammals.

Like whales, like humans.

Printz was a sportsman. He jumped. He ran. Printz is not sluggish.

I was a sportsman. I can be sluggish if I want. Sometimes I like to be sluggish. If I want, I can also be swift.

Rhinos live twenty-five years, sometimes even forty. If they reach forty, they are old and half-blind. They have cataracts. Their hide becomes shriveled and heavy like an elephant's when dung gets stuck on it. When they are old they accumulate too much skin.

Enough about rhinos!

I'm fifty years old. Like a middle-aged rhino. My skin is smooth. My skin is soft and glowing. I'm still a bit handsome.

Printz has no cataracts. Printz has fine eyes, black, slanting. Printz is somehow exotic, and his skin is white. Printz is as tall as a tall Japanese man. Printz is strong. Oh, how handsome and tranquil he is as he watches the rhinos in the late autumn in the empty, completely empty, zoo of a dead city. Printz has not gone gray. Printz has black hair, neatly cut. Printz takes care of it. A good haircut is crucial to him.

Nothing is crucial to me, but I don't realize that yet. Nothing is crucial to me.

His hands are strong. His skin is smooth, it is not dry. It is shiny, shiny. Printz has style. There is no sun now, it is autumn, late autumn, it is very cold and the funeral is over.

Rhinos become sexually mature in their seventh year. Some rhi-nos reach sexual maturity later, but certainly by nine. Female rhinos mature earlier. When they are four, or six years old at the latest.

I matured early, I, Printz. I'm going home. I'm sick of rhinos.

---------------------✂----------------------

Take your panties off, says Printz. *Take your panties off, Maristella, and show me your bum.*

The street goes downhill, it is elegant, it is wide, on both sides there are villas with gardens, with fenced gardens, that stand and watch, silently. Those villas are older than the new country, which after the Second World War became shared and fraternal, among them there is a palace. It is a quiet street away from the center of town, inhabited by important people, political people, because such are the times, political. It is the nineteen-fifties. The street goes downhill and is vaulted with yellow and white blossom, those are trees with yellow and white blooms through which the sky penetrates. This is where Printz lives. Here, in this yellow and white street is also where Maristella lives, with her knobbly knees, her sock that has slipped under her right heel so she is limping, although she is not lame. Maristella has wide-set eyes, blue. They are on their way to the kindergarten at the end of the street that goes downhill and Printz tells Maristella *take off your panties and show me your bum*. They are five years old. Maybe six. They speak clearly. They are healthy and beautiful. He and Maristella.

His name is Printz. Affectionately known as Pupi. He does not like that, he does not like being Pupi, he thinks of himself exclusively as Printz.

Maristella and Printz love each other, that is why it is not terrible when Printz tells Maristella *take off your panties*. Maristella trusts Printz. They go into the garden of the villa called Samantha, the gate is heavy but there is no dog in the garden so it is safe. The barberries are in bloom, the garden is dotted with yellow. The grass is expansive, green, tended, it is a rich garden, in it lies a great spring silence, a morning silence. The grass is scattered with yellow barberry bushes, there is calm in the grass. It is nice. The air is clean. Maristella and Printz hold hands, Maristella has short sleeves and little golden patches on her arms.

You've got little stars on your body, says Printz to Maristella.

And my face, says Maristella.

So your face shines like little stars, Printz smiles, *show me your bum.*

I'm Mama's little star, Mama's little stella, says Maristella.

Show me your bum, says Printz again.

Maristella crouches behind a barberry bush and takes off her panties, Printz says *I can't see, lie down,* Maristella lies down. Her knees are knobbly and scabbed. Maristella climbs trees, especially when the cherries are ripe, that is why she has knobbly, scabbed knees, because she keeps falling. There are five cherry trees in Maristella's garden. There are Morello cherries too. There are three plum trees and four apple trees. There is all kinds of fruit, Printz and Maristella eat fruit when it is ripe and Maristella climbs high up and is grubby. And she kneels on the branches. She climbs down the trees, yelling like an Indian as she climbs down.

Maristella lies down.

Open your legs, I want to see what it's like inside. That is what Printz says.

Maristella lies on the green grass, barberry flowers fall over her face, covering the little stars on her cheeks.

You've got a little ball inside there, says Printz. *It's small and pink.*

That's the vagina, Maristella tells Printz. *That's what my Mama says.*

Your vagina is pink, Printz accepts what Maristella says. He believes her because he loves her. *I'd like to touch it,* says Printz.

Go on then, whispers Maristella.

Printz stretches out his index finger and slowly approaches Maristella's little ball and touches it the way dandelion seeds waft through the air.

It tickles, says Maristella, *we have to go to kindergarten.*

It's run away, says Printz in surprise. *Your little ball's hiding.*

---- ✂ ----

Printz takes off Ernestina's panties. He wipes her, wipes her in front and behind, it depends whether Ernestina has peed or pooed, pissed or crapped. Then he washes her. He places her on the bed, as big as she is, fat as she is and says *open your legs* and (with a small moist towel, light blue) wipes between her flabby buttocks, between her flaccid labia with their dramatically thinned pubic hairs. The opera singer Ernestina has not sung for a long time. A little lump, a mammogram, an operation, radiation. The pains come and go. They spread toward her neck, her fingers grow numb. The pains are called metastases. The pains come when the metastases come to life and drill. Ernestina is fat, Ernestina sweats and speaks loudly, Ernestina is seventy. Her husband, the chemist Rikard Dvorsky, feeds her. Rikard Dvorsky is old, older than his wife Ernestina. Rikard Dvorsky has occasional attacks of amnesia. His speech is sometimes confused, as though a secret inner hand had turned off the light somewhere then turned it on again. Feeding Ernestina irritates Rikard Dvorsky. He no longer calls her Tina, just Ernestina, and shoves food into her mouth tetchily. Ernestina does not have a chance to swallow it before Rikard thrusts the next mouthful at her. Ernestina has started to refuse. She spits out what Rikard tetchily pushes between her half-closed teeth with his fingers. These meals are less appetizing by the day, Rikard cooks but Rikard's nerves are fraying. All this, Ernestina's illness, has been going on too long. The food is pigswill and it makes Ernestina-Tina sick. Her arms hang at the edge of the table like two dead fish on their backs, white-bellied, fattened and stiff, and she is hunched over with unwillingness. At the table, no one speaks. Tina does not speak because she cannot, because her mouth is constantly full. Rikard does not speak because he is angry and afraid. Printz does not speak because neither Tina nor Rikard wants to listen to him anymore, *stop talking,* they say.

--------------------------✂------------------------

Printz quietly opens the door. His father is sitting in a pink arm-chair, switched off. The armchair is covered in pink velour, that is why it is pink. The armchair is fifty years old, or more. It has been dragged through the Dvorskys' life, regularly reupholstered. It came with the house into which Comrade Rikard and Comrade Ernestina Dvorsky moved in 1948. So the prewar life of the pink armchair will be forever unknown; all that is known is its postwar life, the postwar life of the pink armchair.

It is dark in the room.

Where've you been? asks Rikard Dvorsky.

Watching rhinos, says Printz. *They're as fat as Mama.*

Rikard Dvorsky is sitting in the armchair.

Printz says: *Tomorrow let's go to the mountains to clear our heads.*

Printz goes to the kitchen, it is a large kitchen, old-fashioned, with a stained concrete floor, with a floor of red, yellow, and white concrete squares. It is a cheerful floor. Printz drinks milk from a jug. Printz adores milk, he drinks a lot of it. He pours a liter of cold milk into himself, standing up, squashing little lumps of curdled cream with his tongue.

Rikard calls to Printz who is standing in the kitchen drinking cold milk: *When we get back, Herzog is going to buy this flat. I've given him permission to buy the flat.*

What will happen to Rikard Dvorsky, what will happen to Printz when Herzog buys the flat? It is not a clever solution.

That's not clever. Where am I supposed to go? Where will Rikard go when Herzog buys this flat? It's a convenient flat, elegant and spacious. It has lots of rooms, it has ornaments, it's a nice flat. What will happen to us?

It's very quiet without Ernestina, says Rikard Dvorsky. *What are we going to do with her things? She's got a lot of things.*

Maristella did not come to the funeral.

------------------------- ✂ -------------------------

The best thing about the kindergarten is the snack. The kindergarten was set up in another villa, adapted for it. There is no furniture for adults, there is furniture for small children. It is kindergarten furniture, for children. The loaves are big and black and weigh two kilograms. The slices are heavy. The jam is a mixture of fruit. Dark. It comes in plastic containers, also big. The margarine comes in boxes. Everything in the kindergarten comes in large packets, not like at home, in little dishes of porcelain or crystal. Some dishes at home are edged with silver, with engravings of vines, silver vines. The slices are heavy because they are big, they are heavy with margarine and jam so they bend, they make a bridge in his hand. That bread is living bread, it moves. You can't see fruit in that jam. Printz is surprised, Printz is little and he is surprised: *Where does the fruit in the fruit jam go to?* It is the fifties.

Don't provoke me! shouts the teacher with a moustache, a deep voice and broad feet.

The teacher is angry and Printz does not know why. Printz does not understand what she is saying.

I don't understand what you're saying, says little Printz.

In the kindergarten they drink milk made from pale yellow powder, they drink diluted dust. They eat powdered eggs. The teachers stink and have hairy legs. The teachers are not beautiful like his mama, like Maristella's mama. Maristella's mama is even more beautiful than his, Printz's mama, who is called Ernestina-Tina, while Maristella's mama is called Alma. In the kindergarten Tito's portrait hangs high up and watches over all the children.

When no jam comes, they send yellow cheese, which everyone calls *Unra's.**

---

* UNRRA: United Nations Relief and Rehabilitation Administration

Is Unra a cow? asks Printz.

The comrade teacher sends Printz to the corner. *You'll stay there as a punishment,* she says.

Printz (looking at the corner, looking at the ceiling, the ceiling is very high, it is an old villa): *I've got a cow in the garden. My cow is called Kata. Her milk isn't dusty. Her milk isn't yellow. Her milk is as white as my eyes when I turn them up.*

The comrade teacher says: *Get lost, you red-bourgeois trash!*

Printz kneels in the corner and listens to the horse-drawn vehicles. The streets have lots of horses and few cars, such are the times. The horse-drawn vehicles rumble because not all the roads are smooth, they are cobbled, and on the carts big aluminium churns full of milk sway. In front of the doors women wait with saucepans in their hands and cold perms on their heads. His mama does not wait outside. His mama, Printz's mama, sings.

Aunty Hilda waits and calls *Pupi, here's the milk, Pupi.* That was before the cow, before his grandpa bought the cow, which they milked in the garden, before Herzog was born.

There are droppings in the streets.

Printz says: *Horses shit balls.*

This is an American ball, says Rikard to Printz. *I bought it for you. Look how shiny it is, look how colorful it is.*

That was before Herzog as well. The first glass marbles were before Herzog too. There was a lot before Herzog. Herzog does not have any unusual events as memories, he just has ordinary things. Herzog does not remember the clay marbles, but he, Printz, remembers everything. Printz has an excellent memory. Herzog has no idea that before the colorful glass marbles there were only those ugly little balls that do not clink, Herzog has no clue that balls were made of rags and hardly bounced, in fact they did not bounce at all, they just rolled. The shiny American ball bounced, it bounced of its own accord.

Printz does not like the American ball and he does not take it to bed with him. Printz takes the rag-ball to bed with him. Aunty Hilda makes the best rag-balls, the very best. She makes them from Rikard's old socks, Rikard has a lot of old socks and keeps buying new pairs, so he has a lot of new socks as well. In general there are lots of socks in the house.

You don't have to keep rag-balls, says Aunty Hilda. *When they wear out, you make new ones.*

You have to look after American balls because they come from far away. That is what Rikard says. *Don't damage this ball,* Rikard says to Printz. *It's an expensive ball and it comes from far away.* Naturally Printz immediately damaged the American ball, the next day it got a hole in it, the air came out, it deflated and lay crumpled up in the garden. Printz had not liked the American ball from the start. Printz does not kick well because he has high shoes that are heavy. They are called Rudos.

Aunty Hilda smells different from Printz's mama. Printz knows, because Aunty Hilda tells him, that it is Black Cat, while Ernestina wears Chanel. Printz likes Black Cat. Black Cat is all around him, it fills the air.

At the kindergarten, the children boast: *We eat bread mash and potato paprikash.*

At home, Printz announces at the table: *I want bread mash too. I don't want meat.*

Rikard gets angry and shouts: *Shame on you! As a punishment, there'll be no supper for you,* and Ernestina nods, she agrees. Ernestina always agrees, so as not to anger Rikard. Printz does not understand why there is so much punishment, why there are so many stern people. In bed he twists a lock of his black hair. Aunty Hilda comes secretly into his room and whispers: *I'll make you bread mash when we're on our own. And I'll take you to the cinema.*

That's what Aunty Hilda says. Then Printz stops twisting the lock of his hair and falls asleep.

The film is called The Stone Flower. The second film is called The Pike's Command.

Printz asks: *What are pikes?*

Predatory fish. Freshwater fish, says Aunty Hilda, *they can be bombardiers as well.*

Printz does not want to ask who is the one in the film giving commands, the fish or the aeroplane, so he does not ask anymore. He just waits. It is dark in the auditorium, while outside it is a sunny Sunday. Printz likes that. The third film is called Baš Čelik. Printz does not like the third film. Printz screams and holds Aunty Hilda's hand.

I don't want to go to the cinema anymore, says Printz.

Aunty Hilda smiles with her red lips: *I'll read you stories,* she says.

Mama doesn't have such red lips, Printz says.

I use Baiser, Baiser is dark red. Baiser means a kiss and it doesn't rub off.

Then Printz says to Aunty Hilda: *Kiss me.*

The children from the kindergarten have cleats on their shoes. Their shoes clatter but Printz's don't, that's why he says: *I want cleats.*

Ernestina says: *cleats are worn by the poor, cleats are primitive.*

Printz never got shoes with cleats.

In the garden, Printz says to Maristella: *Cut off your plaits. Bobbed hair is fashionable now.*

He also says: *I'm going to be a sculptor.* He says that while he and Maristella dig tunnels in her garden so that the moles can come out, after Maristella screamed:

They'll suffocate under the earth in the pitch dark, liberate the moles, Pupi.

I'm going to be a sculptor, Pupi says again, carrying on digging.

They wait for hours by the holes, no moles come out, only worms.

You're not going to be a sculptor, says the secret agent and chemist Rikard Dvorsky. *You'll work with me, we need people we can trust. You'll be a chemist in the service of the state.*

That is how Printz became a chemist.

-------------------------✂-------------------------

Maristella has an exhibition in New York.

Printz does not own an flat. Printz lives with Rikard, his father, because he does not have an flat and he does not have the money to rent even a small one. Besides, this is more comfortable. It is more secure. It is protected and Printz needs protection even though he is no longer little.

I'd like to be little.

Printz did have an flat of his own, oh yes. Printz was given a socialist flat in socialist days and then he left it to Selena, who now has Printz's socialist flat even though socialism has left. Selena spends most of the time in that flat lying down because she is drunk and there is no one to buy her stockings and she cannot go out without stockings because it is cold outside and her legs are full of broken capillaries, of varicose veins. She has no sheets on the bed, no pillowcase on the pillow. Selena's clothes hang in the bathroom, all her clothes, skirts and sweaters and blouses, and they are ironed by the steam.

Selena has hair as thin as down, reddish. One day Selena will wake up and she'll be bald. I'll buy her stockings so that she can walk through the city bald, in black stockings. Selena is bald because of hormones, her hormones are abandoning her, disappearing. When their hormones disappear, people crumple. My hormones occasionally go away as well, but they come back. Without hormones people grow darker, especially women. Selena was lovely when she had hormones. We won't drink together anymore. I'll buy her black stockings when this passes, this postdeath situation.

It will not pass, Pupi.

Maristella, where are you, Maristella!

Selena lies on Pupi's bed, on Pupi's bed with no bedclothes, in laddered nylons, wearing sunglasses so the light does not bother her. She lies in her flat with two double windows, looking out at a gas station and a little park where dog owners walk their pets twice a day, in a circle. She lies and looks at Pupi's books, which she does not read. There are all kinds of books there, expensive ones.

Enough!

Selena lies in black stockings with ladders in them, surrounded by empty bottles, she lies like that and says out loud: *Ernestina has died and I don't have stockings for the funeral. Funerals require black stockings.*

From the park beneath the window comes damp air, smelling of urine. *I've wet myself,* says Selena.

Socialism refuses to give Printz another flat. Printz buys a flat, a small one. Soon afterward, Printz leaves that flat to Milena. Milena is Printz's second wife. Printz likes getting married. It is a ceremonial act. Milena has two children although those children are not his, Printz's children. *I can't live with you anymore,* Printz says to Milena after a year or two, it doesn't matter which, and goes, leaving her the flat, because what would Milena do without an flat, where would she go? Now Printz has no wardrobe. He has no books. Printz is fifty and he no longer works. Why does he not work?

They sent a letter. They said, thank you, you will get a pension. That pension is small, miserable.

Life abandoned him silently, his life slunk away secretly, without warning, Printz was not ready, he did not hear a thing, he had no idea.

What's this? Some kind of recapitulation? Shoo!

I have to take care of Tina, my mama, says Printz to Maristella who shouts *Pupi, you're crazy!*

When Mama Tina dies, I'll have to take care of Rikard. I've got my hands full. When it's all over, I'll decide what to do. That is what Printz says. *The flat is large, there are things to sell. I'll see,* says Printz.

------------------------ ✂ ------------------------

There are a lot of silver trays in the flat. They are big trays with decorated handles that curl as though they were whining, coil like tiny snakes, they hold at least a dozen glasses, crystal of course. They are trays for liveried waiters but there are no liveried waiters. Some handles are curled like coils of women's hair, some like vines. They are heavy trays from the Villa Nora. When guests come, Rikard and Ernestina Dvorsky take out special cutlery, also silver. The forks are big, the spoons are big, so are the knives. The cutlery is obviously old.

Pupi takes a bag.

Samsonite.

He fills the bag with silverware, silverware that Printz's brother Herzog has not yet taken because it would have been awkward for him to have taken everything at once, that is what Herzog thought. There's time, Herzog decided.

I'm leaving the menorah, I'm leaving the menorah as a memento. It holds seven long slender candles.

The dealer takes out the trays, dishes, cutlery. He takes them out slowly and turns them over in his hands. He runs his index finger over the monogram engraved on each article, runs it tenderly, as though stroking it. The monogram is HL. *Fifty years have passed,* he says. *It's impossible to trace the owner.* This takes place in a small flat in the suburbs. In stuffy half-darkness, in secret. *There are a lot of surnames beginning with "L,"* says the dealer.

Leder, says Printz. *I've looked into it.*

That's leather in German, says the dealer.

Leder—the owners of the Villa Nora. My information is very reliable. Are there descendants, look into that, find out.

I'll do what I can, promises the dealer.

If you don't get anywhere, melt it all down, melt it all and feed the beggars, says Printz and leaves.

At home, Ernestina, irradiated with cobalt, shrieks: *All my silver's gone! My own son has robbed me! I've been nurturing a snake in my bosom!*

Rikard Dvorsky has a blackout and says nothing.

Printz drinks milk, he always drinks milk when there's electricity in the air. Printz drinks milk and says: *I'll comb Tina's wig.* And he says: *I'm going to comb your wig, Mama, then you can sing.*

---------------------✂-----------------------

It is very cold but the Dvorsky family is cheerful. The Dvorsky family is healthy and young and asleep. And they no longer live in the Villa Nora. It is 1975. The city is shrouded in snow. It is night. Printz takes two suitcases

Samsonite

and leaves the flat. The flat is warm. Printz is wearing a nice jacket, fur, inside-out lambskin. The jacket is yellowish-brown and expensive. Printz has leather gloves lined with rabbit fur and high shoes lined with rabbit fur. Rabbit fur is soft and Printz's toes are melting with rabbit softness.

I'm wrapped in animals, says Printz. *I'm wrapped in dead animals. That's the fashion,* he says.

The Dvorsky family does not live in the Villa Nora any longer as the Villa Nora has been transformed into the residence of a nonaligned ambassador, maybe Egyptian, maybe Sudanese, if the

Sudan was nonaligned. It was the age of nonalignment.

Printz carries the suitcases as though he is going on a trip, he carries them in an official manner. Printz goes to the railway station but it is late, it is very late, there are no trains. There are homeless people in the corners, on the wet station floor, spat on, peed on. The homeless people doze as though they are waiting. Some of them drink beer. The station is half dark.

Printz sits down on the threshold of the waiting room, in front of it, because the waiting room is locked just so as to stop the homeless people warming themselves inside. *Just for that reason,* says Printz. Printz shouts *Come!* and the homeless people, men and women, draw near. The homeless people are dirty and neglected. And dishevelled.

I've brought clothes. And food, says Printz, opening the suitcases. The homeless people drag, snatch and stuff things into their plastic bags, for the homeless always have plastic bags because it is all they have.

There aren't any coats here, says a woman.

We can swap, he says, taking off his jacket of inside-out lambskin, yellowish brown, and putting on a thin lightweight coat covered in stains, crumpled. *The sleeves are too short for me,* says Printz.

Printz goes home with empty hands, without gloves lined with rabbit fur. Printz skips through the white landscape, nocturnal, whistling.

I feel light and cheerful.

The Dvorsky family is asleep. Printz goes to the kitchen and drinks three glasses of cold milk. Then he falls asleep in the pink armchair.

------------------------------ ✂ ------------------------------

Printz opens out his folding camp bed. *We'll go away tomorrow,* he says. *We're going away tomorrow, Papa.*

Maybe I shouldn't have let Herzog have this flat? Rikard Dvorsky wonders but no one responds. Printz says nothing or else he is asleep.

The curtains are not often washed, nor are the windows. The drapes are made of heavy satin, pink like the armchair. The rooms are bathed in opaque light, dense light that does not flicker but sticks to objects, pressing on them. It is a cold light that comes in slyly through small cracks.

-----------------------✂-----------------------

Ernestina lies like rolled-out dough in the room of white wood run through with gold threads. The mirrors are crystal, of course, and there are three of them, one on the dressing table, two on the wardrobe doors. Ernestina is sleeping, she sleeps because the morphine injections are ever stronger, ever stronger, and she dreams, she dreams in bright colors that she is singing in the town where Maristella is currently exhibiting her paintings, oh, that bitch Maristella (and her mother Alma) abandoned Printz to go and buy little flats for unknown cunts.

At night father and son, Rikard and Printz Dvorsky, go into the study with bookshelves stretching across two walls, and over a whiskey they look at each other, watching a world disappear, their world, after which comes nothing, while the ice in their crystal glasses clinks and the flower pots flake, dry and rotten.

Printz is asleep.

I'm not asleep.

Printz is lying on a narrow camp bed beside the dining table, the table is long, made of rosewood and it has slender legs, ending in little lion paws. Printz is covered with a checked blanket, it is warm in the flat. Printz is not wearing pyjamas, it is silly to put on pyjamas when you are sleeping on a camp bed beside the dining table, it is silly to take your socks off. Printz's socks are dry; after the rain at the funeral, after the rain at the zoo, they dried. Printz has black socks, knee-high, formal socks, for the opera and funerals—a blend of cotton and silk, expensive men's socks.

Rikard Dvorsky lies in the double bed where his wife, the fat opera singer Ernestina-Tina, died and says: *We're going to the mountains tomorrow, Printz and I.*

---------------------✂---------------------

Female rhinos carry their young for fifteen months.

Mama Ernestina-Tina says, *nine months, that's an age.*

It is the winter of 1950 and Herzog is being born. Everyone is waiting for Herzog. Grandpa and Grandma come from another city, also large, also old, also a capital. In the shared country there are several main cities but one main main city. The Dvorsky family comes from a smaller main city and was moved to the main main city because it was deserving. Grandpa sells one of his houses: Grandpa is a businessman and he has more than enough houses and shops. Grandpa sells a house and buys a cow so that Herzog has milk. *It's better not to have a lot of houses,* whisper the family round the engraved table, *they'll get taken from you in any case.* Grandpa has never had a cow before, he does not know anything about cows, he does not know how to milk them. Grandpa puts the cow in the garden behind the Villa Nora because Nora is the name of the villa in which Printz is now living.

When Printz was on the way, they did not sell anything big, just little things, and there was a lot of poverty, postwar. Printz was born in a Catholic city, then they moved to an Orthodox city. He was little. Printz was not baptized as either Catholic or Orthodox—that is all right. That does not bother Printz. Had he been baptized into any faith, Printz would have rejected it by now. When Printz was born, books were sold. And some clothes. It was 1946. Printz's grandmother waited in line for one egg, for one hollow bone to make soup. She waited all morning, the lines were long. It was 1947. Printz's grandmother whisks the egg with sugar, it is disgusting, she gives half to Printz, half to Maristella. Printz and Maristella eat whisked egg yolk in postwar poverty because Printz and Maristella were born in the same lesser main city and were moved at the same time to the main main city because their fathers had the same duties, State and secret.

Open your mouth, says Printz's grandmother, *here's something lovely.* Printz is obedient, Printz has always been obedient, he opens his mouth because neither he nor Maristella can talk yet. They know how to cry and laugh. Printz's grandmother has a soft chin that wobbles.

The theaters are full, Mama Tina sings and she is very fat while little Herzog has a big nose and fair hair. And light-colored eyes. Herzog is Printz's brother. They do not look alike. They tell Printz—*stay here, we're going to bring you a brother.* They leave him for two days. He waits. He waits outside, by the door. Aunty Hilda wears a lacy apron, it is very small, as though meant for Maristella's dolls. Aunty Hilda has a little white cap. The cap is small as well. Aunty Hilda opens and closes the front door, looks out, makes sure that he, Printz, is there. Where else would he be? He is four years old, they told him to wait *wait, we're going to bring you a brother.* He waits, and it is snowy outside. The garden is deep in snow and it sparkles. It is quiet waiting in the snow, in front of the thick front door, brown, with a yellow knocker in the middle. The knocker is the brass head of a troll with bulging eyes. Aunty Hilda says: *You'll freeze, Pupi. I want to see my brother,* says Printz, adding: *don't call me Pupi. I'm Printz.* They are coming. The car is gray and called an Opel. There are not many gray Opels around. Mama Tina sits on the edge of the bed, the curtains are flowery, Herzog suckles, Printz touches, Tina shouts: *Don't touch!* Printz touches, Mama Tina shouts *don't touch, don't ever touch either him or me!* Printz's fingers burn.

It is 1950. They tell Printz, they keep repeating, constantly repeating: *remember this,* they say. *Remember this street, remember the number of the house, 23, remember, your name is Printz Dvorsky, your mama is called Ernestina-Tina and your papa Rikard. Mama sings at the opera, papa is a chemist at the Institute. Say that if you ever get lost, don't ever wander off on your own. Aunty Hilda is here. The street is called Tito Street.* And then they say: *Your brother is called Herzog.*

Herzog has a big nose, he is big all over, a big baby, with green snot dripping from his nose.

---------------------------✂----------------------------

Perhaps it is 1953. It is winter again and again there is a lot of snow. Everyone is shrieking, even Aunty Hilda, who never shrieks. *Where's Herzog!* the people in the house yell, running up and down. The Villa Nora has two staircases. It goes on for a long time, that searching through the house, the house is full of hidden places. Printz is wearing yellow pyjamas with little bears printed haphazardly on them, he has brown slippers on his bare feet. Printz goes to the garden shed. The cow is there but no Herzog. The hens are asleep. The snow is wet. Printz leaves the garden and sets off along the yellow street that is now white because the trees are bare so the whiteness is reflected from the sky. Printz does not look up. Up there it can be dark and Printz is afraid. At the top of the street is the main road. Printz walks along the deserted main road alone, in his yellow pyjamas, it is very quiet. Printz walks, twisting a lock of his black hair. Printz is seven. Printz walks for a long time. His feet are wet, he has no socks on, only small slippers. The main road is decorated with shops. Some shops have lights on, some do not, but all the shops are poor because it is 1953, under socialism. The shop windows are filled with various tiny objects, so that passersby can see what is inside. There is food, sausages and small chocolate bars, expensive, there are books with various drawings, there are New Year decorations, rubber slip-on shoes, bales of cretonne, knitted hats, garden spades and forks, there is the occasional toy, wooden. In early socialism there are no shops with specific things, and there are no glass marbles or lacquered balls and the notebooks are thin. The shops are collective and they are called stores.

Printz's walk lasts a long time. Then, at the end of the main road, far from the Villa Nora, very far, Printz comes to a shop window in great disorder and says: *Let's go home, Herzog*. Printz's lips are black with cold, Herzog's nose is running with thick green snot and they toddle off down the street towards the Villa Nora, soaking wet. There is no one anywhere.

I'll kill you! shouts Mama Tina, looking at Printz while she dresses Herzog.

----------------------- ✂ -----------------------

Rhinos live in bare places, isolated places, and they roam. Sometimes they run in a panic, as though demented.

Rhino horns are not real horns, they do not grow out of the skull. They are soft horns, made of matter like nails, like hair. Rhinos travel alone. When they give birth to little rhinos, that is the only time they are not alone. The mothers take care of the little rhinos until a new little rhino is born. Then the mothers abandon the first little rhino, saying: now you are grown up, off you go. The first little rhino is still small although it is bigger than the new rhino, just born, which is very small and helpless. So, rhinos roam alone, because the mothers cannot manage several little rhinos at the same time. Mother rhinos can only be bothered with one baby, not with two.

-------------------- ✂ --------------------

Come out, screams Mama Ernestina-Tina. Ernestina has a penetrating voice. When she screams *Come out!* it is as though she were in the theater on the stage. She has spread her legs wide, everything is wet. Beside the bed stands Maristella's mother Alma, stroking Tina's forehead and whispering *it'll be all right, Tina, everything will be all right. Push.* Maristella's mother Alma is not yet fat but she soon will be because five months later Maristella will be born.

Oh, Maristella, where are you!

His mother is very fat. She is bathed in sweat and steaming. There is a lot of noise outside. His mother is angry. That outside din upsets him, it is quite all right inside. On Ernestina's upper lip moisture gathers in little drops that glisten. Those little drops keep collecting. And when she died, when she stopped breathing, her nostrils glistened. That disgusted Printz. He did not like Ernestina kissing him because then she passed her moistness onto him, onto his face. He always wiped it off.

Printz, who would later be called Pupi, does not want to come out. He refuses. Ernestina strains, so does Printz. Ernestina pushes, Printz uses his tiny hands to hold onto the slippery walls of the inside and goes back into the darkness, turning his head away, there is a painful brightness outside. Printz presses his lips into a hard, crinkled "o." They are little lips as blue as a plum.

Plums cost 50 dinars in 1946.

They are tiny lips pressed into a bud, tightly pressed together as though protecting themselves from sourness.

70

A lemon cost 100 dinars in 1946.

Printz uses his wrinkled feet to press against the walls of velvety darkness because his hands are no longer enough. He turns pale blue, dark blue, black. Nothing flows, only his great resistance drums, Printz is suffocating. Printz wants to lose consciousness so that he does not have to come out, ever.

They pull him out by force.

He is pulled out by a family friend, the vet Oto. Oto says: *calves are easier to deliver than your baby, Tina.* The family vet never comes to visit again. The Dvorsky family moves to a different city, and when the cow, with two pigs and seven bare-necked hens that lay speckled eggs moved into the long street, into the garden behind the Villa Nora, a vet used to come who was not allowed into the drawing room.

The blanket is soft, it is dark in the blanket.

They leave Printz to get warm. Printz quivers because he is angry.

That is how Printz was born.

That's how I, Printz, was born.

Printz's baby carriage stands beside Maristella's for a photograph. Maristella's baby carriage is elegant, big and high, her baby carriage is white. Maristella has a little cap on her head and a bright knitted jacket. Maristella is like a doll. Maristella's clothes are pink, maybe yellow, maybe light blue, you cannot tell from the photograph because it is not a color photograph. There is snow on the ground. The hardness of the ground can be sensed. His baby carriage looks old. Printz is wrapped in a dark blanket of rough material and he is cold, that is obvious from the photograph. Printz is squinting. Maristella is laughing. Maristella is toothless and she is laughing. Printz is looking straight ahead, at what, we don't know. Printz is not laughing. It is snowing. Then they are moved.

Tina gets fatter and sings. *It's because of Printz,* Tina repeats at every meal. They have lunch at an oval table. Aunty Hilda circles round the table, she is new. Aunty Hilda does not take her little cap off. The little cap sticks up, like a cockerel's crest, only white.

Printz has fallen asleep.

Yes, I've fallen asleep.

---------------------------✄----------------------

Printz has a brother.

We've said that. I have a brother.

His brother is called Herzog,

Herz—heart. He's not as handsome as me and he can't be called Printz.

Herzog lives with his wife and children in the same building, on the same floor, in a flat whose walls adjoin the walls of Rikard Dvorsky's flat. Herzog has little fish and a Rottweiler, black. He has ornaments and works of art. Little silver ornaments, small ashtrays, dishes for sweets, ivory elephants, tusks, crystal plates and vases, he has lace doilies, he has a huge Buddha made of sandalwood who sits, cross-legged, behind the front door and is all golden and fragrant.

I brought Herzog the Buddha, from Burma.

He has Persian rugs.

Herzog keeps gradually and silently transferring the ornaments, the paintings and the carpets from Rikard Dvorsky's flat to his small one across the hall. For two years Herzog carries things away, while his mother, the former opera diva Ernestina Dvorsky, née Bosner, lies in a morphine landscape, blissfully. That small flat, very convenient as it is right here, next door, was bought for Herzog by his father Rikard Dvorsky, retired scientist and intelligence officer who had long ago published a collection of patriotic, somewhat pugnacious, poems, which no one remembers anymore.

What am I going to do, asks Printz, *I've nowhere to go.*

In the course of two years, Herzog Dvorsky's small flat has become even smaller and then overnight it has grown cramped. There are too many things in it. There is no space in it for Herzog Dvorsky's family because Herzog Dvorsky's family is growing, spreading, becoming fatter. Herzog is big and pale, he was always pale, he was born pale,

and big, I was not born, they pulled me out,

the green snot no longer drips from his nose because when it comes he swallows it. There is no space for Herzog's wife Matilda, known as Tilda, it is cramped for his children (Herzog has two children, also big and fat); there is no space for the little fish because the aquarium is huge although the little fish keep eating each other so there are fewer of them; the Rottweiler almost jumps up at the chandelier, it is so powerful. And unruly.

What about the flowers? Herzog has lots of flowers on his pink balcony. His wife Tilda likes pink. All the flowers are pink. The flowers face the street, the street is noisy, but the flowers live, they even bloom. Pinkly.

Herzog's wife looks like young Ernestina. It seems to Printz that he and Herzog have two mamas, one old, one young;

Ernestina is no more, only the copy that does not sing is left.

It seems to Printz that Rikard has two wives, one old, one young. It is muddled. Herzog's wife is called Matilda but known as Tilda. She is as fat as Ernestina, who is known as Tina. She talks as loudly as Ernestina. She is cheerful

she's acting

she is kind

she's not

her belly shakes when she walks and goes to the market every day.

Call me Tilda, says Matilda as she turns round in front of the mirror in Ernestina's stage dresses. Yes, Tilda wears Ernestina's dresses because—they fit her. Sometimes she adjusts them, sometimes she does not. They are evening dresses, made of brocade and lamé, of silk and taffeta, red, black, lacy, transparent, shot through with silver thread and gold thread, fluttery with pastel voile, long, with a deep décolleté

so her tits show.

Matilda has big tits. Matilda has the same hairstyle as Ernestina. She has brown hair and blue eyes.

It is very confusing. Perhaps the two women have a plan. Printz is confused. Matilda does not sing. Nor does Ernestina sing anymore. Ernestina only sweats. Ernestina is dead.

So, Printz and Herzog are brothers and they love each other.

No.

Sleep, Pupi. And take your socks off.

Printz loves Herzog.

Mr. Rikard Dvorsky, retired chemist and communist, speaks French, Italian and English from his youth.

When he was in the Partisans those languages made him suspect, he was also suspect because of his degree in chemistry, but he survived, he was even awarded a badge. Later, because of that badge, he got credit for a car on hire purchase, interest-free for five years.

I would have bought the car for that credit, says Printz, who is already a mature chemist with a wife. *No way,* chirps Ernestina-Tina, *Herzog will buy the car.*

---------------------------✂-----------------------------

After the war (1948), Rikard Dvorsky is advised (ordered) to move into the Villa Nora. *Sit there and wait for directives,* they say. Villa Nora is a furnished villa in a long street, going downhill like a mountain path. The bedrooms are upstairs. Printz sleeps on his own and there is no Herzog yet. Afterward Printz sleeps on his own and Herzog with his mother. Rikard learns new languages at night, downstairs in the living room. Printz goes downstairs in his pyjamas, he has hair as black as a raven's

while Herzog's is fair and curly

Herzog is born later

little Printz goes downstairs, twisting a lock of his hair between his right thumb and forefinger, twists it and goes down drowsily.

This is Russian, Pupi, says the chemist Rikard Dvorsky.

Printz says: *I want some milk.*

Rikard Dvorsky brings Printz a glass of cold milk, *I want a bottle of milk,* says Printz.

Printz drinks a liter of cold milk straight off and he is very little. Life is good.

Ernestina sings on the radio, she sings at the opera, she performs in nurseries and old people's homes, in factory halls. She is paid between 367 and 953 dinars. Rikard works in the Institute, he works on medicaments, but he is told: *you work for us and it will remain secret.* So Rikard works for the secret service. That is before Printz asks *what about me, where shall I go?* A long time before. Printz is small, he gulps the milk and twists the lock of his raven hair, always the same one, on his right temple. Later they will be moved.

They've moved us into this flat here. A city flat. They've moved Maristella as well.

----------------------✂----------------------

Printz twitches in his sleep. The camp bed is short, rickety and narrow. The thin checked blanket slips off.

That's why it's better not to take one's socks off, that's why.

Half-asleep Printz listens. The door of the bedroom where Rikard Dvorsky, the once powerful informer, sleeps curled up on the big bed is open and no longer white. It is a sickly yellow door, yellowish-gray, in fact dirty, especially around the handle. Round the handle there are stains of spinach, of porridge, of unwashed hands. There are red stains of rouge for the face, with which Ernestina tries to conceal her inner and outer grayness, her lurking death.

Pupi, bring me my makeup and put color on my cheeks. And my eyelashes, Pupi. And my eyelashes.

But Ernestina does not have any eyelashes. Eyelashes fall off with radiation. Then the eyes are left bare and very round.

The walls are not white anymore either. For two years the walls have been sucking in the decay exhaled at them.

Rikard Dvorsky withdraws to the edge of the bed as though he was fleeing from the invisible but existing Ernestina. Lying on his side, he looks at the neon light through the half-lowered blinds, it is quiet outside, the night is deep. What will he do now?

Printz waits. Printz waits for his Mama Tina to call him, *Pupi, the toilet, quick, Pupi.* Tina groans, Pupi leaps up, he does everything required. What does he do? He takes off Ernestina's underwear, puts them on the toilet shelf, goes away, comes back, wipes her, wipes her in front and behind, it depends whether Ernestina is peeing or pooing, pissing or crapping. Then he washes her. He places her on the bed, big as she is, fat as she is and says *open your legs,* and (with a little moist towel) wipes between her flabby buttocks, between her flabby labia with their dramatically thinned pubic hair, he washes the woman who gave birth to him with a curse.

He does not touch anything.

Only Rikard Dvorsky moans softly in the double bed.

Have they burned Tina yet? Maybe they burn people collectively. In bulk. What are those ovens like? I'll go and see. I'll go and see what the ovens where dead people are burned look like.

What about the coffins? Do they burn the coffins as well? There are some very expensive coffins. I'm interested in that. Perhaps that's what interests me most now—do they burn the coffins?

---------------------✂----------------------

(the black notebook)

Printz keeps an exercise book for notes under his pillow. When he folds up his camp bed (and he does so increasingly rarely), the notebook is left locked inside with the squashed days like cramped ghosts.

It is an old exercise book, half a century old, big, with a hard cover. The cover is wrapped in black canvas and is stained with time, there are holes in it, which fray. The canvas has been corroded by damp, neglect and forgetfulness. There are unused pages in the notebook, which Printz uses to note down his ideas because Printz is inundated with cascades of ideas that he wants to tame. Between 1946 and 1950 Rikard and Ernestina Dvorsky had recorded the income and outgoings that determined their life. The notebook is like an enigmatic mirror of the past, in it the postwar period is glimpsed through the price of provisions, items bought and sold, in it days are reduced to headwords and then only some days. Other days are not there. The years are compressed into columns, numbers. Printz likes that, that distance, that starkness. This exercise book is part of his past, a past that is not remembered and that is why he needs the notebook, to remember. Printz.

I love this notebook.

Printz was born in 1946, but in the notebook he is hardly mentioned. There is a brief, roundabout reference: baby carriage, secondhand, 1125 dinars, bought on 3 December

but I was already six months old.

You didn't take me for walks when I was little, says Printz to Rikard Dvorsky in the course of their nocturnal conversations in the library while they waited for Tina's departure.

Each time Rikard Dvorsky would wave his hand: *Don't confabulate,* he said.

In January 1947 (19 January) they buy medicine for Printz and take him to the doctor. That costs 150 dinars. Five days later (24 January 1947), they pay 97 dinars to have his ear examined.

You were born with a hole in your ear, says Rikard Dvorsky.

Printz: *Which ear?*

Rikard does not remember. He thinks it was on the outer ear, behind. *The hole was sewn up,* he says, *don't worry.*

Photographs of the wedding—580 dinars (January 1946).

Printz was born in June.

I already existed at the wedding, Printz tries to remember, every night he tries to remember because nobody remembers any longer the way it is recorded in the notebook. No one remembers him.

Perhaps I hiccuped. People drink at festivities. I must have hiccuped in Tina's stomach, fetuses get hiccups, that's a well-known fact.

Lying on the camp bed by the table, almost under the table, like a dog in a kennel, Printz leafs through the black notebook every night as though it was a prayer book. Tonight he gets up, feels his way through the darkness so as not to wake Tina, correction, not to wake Rikard, he gets up, goes in his socks to the kitchen, over whose cheerful floor cockroaches scuttle. City cockroaches are the biggest and fattest cockroaches, his socks are sticky,

Rikard drops honey on the kitchen floor, his hand shakes,

instead of going into the porcelain dish with the gold rim, instead of going into the cup waiting on the marble board under the window, the honey drips onto the floor this morning, before the funeral,

careful, Papa, the honey's dripping

this morning, a long time ago, the precise hand of Rikard Dvorsky surrendered

leave me alone, I don't care about the honey

you've wet yourself, Pa, you've peed in your pyjamas

his father's flaccid willy peers out of his open fly, his father's willy with no hairs, brown—when he pees, he pees haphazardly

who's going to clean it up now, we'll have to get a woman to clean, Papa,

to clean what?

Printz gently taps one sticky smear then another, as though he was dancing. That cheers him up. Printz opens the fridge and standing there drinks milk, two liters of milk, he drinks up all the milk in the fridge, illuminated by the light of the little bulb in the huge stone kitchen, entirely dark, always dark, in the stone kitchen that looks out at the street light. From the edge of his lips, down his chin—in mischievous streams run little white roads that cross like small lively snakes, benign, like grass snakes—and fall onto his chest.

That cools, oh how nicely that cools.

Printz goes back to the dining room, perhaps he should wash the kitchen floor, it is four o'clock in the morning, he will not wash the floor, Printz sits down in the pink armchair, switches on a small lamp—40 watts, and tears out page after page.

I'm tidying the past. I'm making space for my thoughts, I have new thoughts, says Printz in the night.

October 1946:

10,000 in the cash-box, Lisa returned 217 (*who's Lisa?*), darning thread and white thread 350, hair oil 150, hairnet 60, socks for Rikard 350, face and hand cream 310, 3 jars of mustard 600 (!!!), a kilo of sweet conserve 240, jam 380, 1 kilo of walnuts 120 (*preparing for a family celebration*), glass for Rikard's clock 45, shoes for Olga 1316 (*who's Olga?*), two pairs of stockings for Tina 501.60, 1 kerchief 135, jumper for Rikard 836, jumper for Tina 585.50, road tax 101, shoes for Tina—957.40, shoes for Toni (*who's Toni?*), silk for underwear for Tina 390 (!?), loan to Ernest (*who's Ernest?*), cash for beggar 20 (*only?*), 300 to Lisa (*Lisa again*), water 106, apples 48, lemons 60, 1 egg 24, 1 kilo of pears 56, 1 kilo of rice 145, skirt, made by dressmaker, 100, sausages, ham and olives 452, padlock 130, 2 tops for Tina 264, 3 pairs of knickers for Tina 234, 6 pairs men's socks (Rikard) 420, washing powder 50, total 11,270.

November 1946:

Receipts: 6000 + 6000.

half a kilo of figs, bus 40, passes 45 (*for what?*), gift for Ada (*who's Ada?*), pictures 80, thread for socks 80 (they get through a lot of socks), 2 kilos oranges 300, cabbage 525 (*how much cabbage?!*), oranges (*again?*) 140, juice (*what sort?*), suit for Rikard 3000, cinema 45, for the canteen (*what about me?*), flowers (*who for? social life*), oranges and mandarins 240, tram 80, 2 kilos of meat 520, 10 eggs 350 (*eggs are going up*), 1 kilo of rice 125 (*they eat a lot of rice—rice has come down*), henna for hair and comb 150, apron 950 (*who for?*), trousers for Rikard 1000, pyjamas and 2 shirts (*no price—they buy a lot of clothing*).

December 1946:

1 tin of meat, 10 tins of fish, 5 kilos of sugar, 2 liters of oil, 1 kilo, altogether 1270 dinars (*preparing for New Year's eve, 1947*), umbrella for Paula (*who's Paula?*), umbrella for Rikard (*a rainy December*), 2 caps and a hat 2600 (expensive), 1 spoon 130 (*why only one?*), cinema and theater 250 (*who looks after me?*), 10 kilos of dried meat (*Heavens!*) 5500 (*Heavens! Half Rikard's salary*), half a kilo of plums (*why do they save on plums?*) 85, 1 kilo of beans 75, for the lift 47.

Perhaps they lied to me? Perhaps my memories are an illusion, perhaps my memories are someone else's memories? Printz wonders, looking at his toes. He takes his left foot to his nose and smiles: *my feet never smell.*

3 kilos of cabbage (*fermented? I don't like sauerkraut*), 1 kilo of spinach 56 (*for me?*), half a kilo of lettuce 30, greens for soup (*for me? I'm a baby*), Papa returned money for children's shoes—1000 (*whose papa?, whose children?*) cakes 240, 10 eggs 240, electricity 27, 6 meters of material (*for sheets?*), gift for Alma 1900.

Maristella was born!

4 pairs of socks, scarf for Rikard 600 (New Year gift?), cap for Olga 400 (*Olga again, who's Olga?*), small bag for Olga 220 (*I didn't get anything*), sale of Rikard's suit—10,000 (*dinner suit?*).

End of the year of Printz's birth.

End of the year of my birth.

In January 1947—three outings to the theater 200 + 100 + 165, for books on two occasions 100 + 520, they buy butter twice—200 + 150, they sell a suit—3,500 (*to whom?*), photographs are developed—380, someone is ill: 280 for medicine, eggs—6 for 90 dinars.

In February 1947 yet another suit of Rikard's is sold for 3,800, a bra costs 160 dinars, 4 eggs and wire 130 (*what kind of wire?*), a haircut 100 dinars, Arsen appears and is given 730 dinars (*who's Arsen?*), butter for Melita (?!) 160, butter "for us" 100, flowers for Melita 375 (*maybe Melita is Maristella's mother Alma?*).

I have a defective memory concludes Printz in the night. Pegs 100, locksmith (*!*), more flowers—350, in February soap is bought, in April two light bulbs for 310 dinars (*why two?*).

It is five o'clock, it is still dark.

In April 1947 a lamb and bits and pieces—500, spinach 15, paint for a cupboard for 1000. April ends with a deficit of 1604 dinars.

In May 1947 Unra appears—one packet 500 dinars, needles (*!?*)—60 dinars and lace 100, 2 ice creams and tram—20 dinars, bread costs 6, Rikard's shoes are repaired twice, for 29 and 30 dinars, they pay into a commune, wine is drunk, eggs come down in price: 10 for 36 dinars, beer is bought by the liter—2 liters: 56 dinars. Shoe polish 8 dinars, a lot of cherries are bought, and calendars (*!*),

and more thread, more lace and 3 kilos of milk powder, flowers cost
only 10 dinars.

Good times. Family times. Communist times, says Printz and by
then it is morning.

------------------------- ✄ -------------------------

In the mountains Printz and Rikard go for walks. The walks bore
them. Their steps are short. The mountain is deserted, the hotel
is deserted, the tablecloths are gray and have holes in them. The
sheets have holes too, stained with rust, and the towels are thin
and frayed. They get soaked straight away. Soaked with what?
They just get soaked.

The trees have no needles, it is a deciduous forest, so a deciduous mountain, thin, sparse as Selena's hair, bald with holes as well.
A low mountain near the city.

On the mountain Printz asks his father: *Why did you take that
little dog away from me?*

You had a cow, says Rikard.

On the mountain they decide: *We won't buy a grave. We'll move
Tina's urn to her hometown. When the roads reopen, when the war is
over.* That is what they decide.

Which war? asks Printz.

Rikard looks at Printz and says: *You'll have me cremated too.
You'll move me back to MY hometown.*

Printz nods and says: *Okay.*

Perhaps Printz would like to say: *Your hometown is in another
country now. Your hometown was attacked by people from this town
here while we watched. My hometown was attacked by people from
this town here and we said nothing and watched. We stayed here because it would have been complicated to leave because Ernestina was
dying. Did it have to be like that. Father? Rikard Dvorsky. Did it have*

to be like that? Perhaps that is what Printz would have liked to say. Perhaps he would have added: *When it all began, you said: I don't think it will be too bad and you sent me to Bali.* Perhaps that is what Printz would have liked to say. But he did not.

That is what Printz is like.

So, when Rikard says: *You'll have me cremated too. You'll move me back to my hometown,* Printz says: *Don't worry, I know all there is to know about urns.*

Rikard asks: *What urns?*

They are obviously talking slowly. Because they are walking. They are walking along mountain paths with no aromas. It is an unimpressive mountain and they are sorry they came.

Printz knows, there are all kinds of urns. There are big ones, double, for married couples, made of mahogany or teak. They are expensive. They are urns for when both die, husband and wife, mother and father, at the same time, but that rarely happens. Oh yes, there are all kinds of urns, Printz has seen. There are some made of hand-crafted glass, they are beautiful, as though they come from Murano: cobalt blue with an elegantly shaped lid the color of amber, opaquely transparent, just enough for the white dust inside to be seen. There are some made of alabaster, shaped like a pyramid, as though they contained the remains of tiny pharaohs. Urns are made of marble, of /various metals, ceramic, wooden, with floral arrangements or with engravings on the front, visible side. On the back there is usually nothing, on the back, urns are smooth. Urns are little statues and they can be made in the shape of a book, in the shape of an open or closed book, according to taste. Some urns are replicas of various pagodas, and some are for pets, those ones are small, even smaller than urns for people which are usually about thirty centimeters high. Pets are smaller than their owners unless they are horses or cows. In the matter of urns, people have let their imaginations run wild and Printz wonders whether somewhere there is perhaps some kind of museum of urns, empty or full, no matter.

The choice of urns is unbelievably wide. You can get them on hire purchase, says Printz.

Printz knows that urns exist in order to protect the living from the dead. He does not want to say that to Rikard. When they are poured into urns, the dead no longer have anything, neither body nor soul. Printz would like to see a soul, he does not know how. He will work on it. That is what he decides as he walks on the mountain over rotting leaves because it is still autumn. All that remain in urns are gold teeth if the deceased had any and they were not stolen. Then urns are gold inside and they twinkle like Disney films, they are full of magic dust. Like Tinkerbell from Peter Pan. Printz adores Tinkerbell from Peter Pan, because she is mischievous, she can be bad. Printz would like that, he would very much like to be bad sometimes.

When widespread diseases rage, people are burned. When they are infectious diseases. Printz knows that. On the mountain, Printz becomes mellow and calls himself Pupi. *Pupi,* says Printz, *people are burned when there are wars and widespread disease, but ghosts are calm, they don't travel, they don't hover, they are silent, oh yes, ghosts are silent.* Printz knows how good the silence of ghosts is, he knows it very well, and he is glad that they burned Tina.

I'm glad that we burned Tina, he says.

It would have been a big coffin, too heavy to be moved to her hometown, especially in wartime. In wartime, it is best for the dead to stay put.

When we get back to the city, I'll have my teeth out, says Rikard.

Printz is captivated by Rikard's teeth. Rikard has his own teeth and he is old. Old people do not usually have their own teeth. Rikard does not have a prosthesis, even a small one, he does not even have a small bridge, and he had white coffee with stale breadcrumbs soaked in it for breakfast until they moved into the Villa Nora. He ate a lot of polenta. Rikard adores polenta. In the Villa Nora the breakfasts changed, every morning oranges were squeezed. Now Rikard's teeth are starting to decay and that bothers him. He wants to remove that unpleasantness at once, at a stroke. That is what Printz's father Rikard is like. Hasty. Printz will have his teeth out as well, that is what he decides, he will have his teeth out when Rikard dies because he will not have the money for dentists, he knows that already, as he walks on the mountain. Printz does not like mountains.

Printz says again *I'm glad that we had Tina burned*—he likes the way it sounds, that he, Printz, is glad. In Bali, cremations are beautiful, festive, with a lot of color, he would like to describe that to his father. His father is called Rikard. That is a stern name, strong. Printz would like to have that: sternness and strength in his name.

In Bali cremations are wonderful, says Printz to Rikard.

We could have bought a more expensive urn, Rikard replies to the mountain air in front of him. Rikard does not want to look at Printz. Rikard is not interested in how things are in Bali: *That tin urn will be corroded over time and it will get little holes in it.* It's very light.

Printz: *In Bali they build a high tower made of wood and bamboo and place their dead in it, then they set fire to the tower then after forty-two days they build a new tower and put dolls big dolls life-sized brightly colored dolls into it and set it on fire again and then they scatter the ash over the water around Bali there's a lot of water because Bali is an island.*

Rikard: *If holes develop in the urn, Ernestina could seep out, like sand.*

Printz: *In Bali there is no word for heaven the main city is called Denpasar and Bali is a heavenly island. There are heavenly ducks there.*

Rikard: *She would trickle out, white, because the ash of the dead is white.*

Printz: *Like Unra milk.*

In Bali I ate roast duck, in Bali they put the duck into a leaf they pick from a banana tree that's a huge leaf very green dark green then they roast it with herbs and roots and they call it bebek betutu that roast duck that's what they call it bebek betutu it's served at ceremonial dinners after canapés of caviar and little tomatoes after champagne I was wearing a white dinner suit like Suharto.

Rikard is tired, he does not want to walk anymore. *I need the toilet,* he says.

Printz is not sure that Rikard hears what he is saying. Printz thinks that his voice carries, that he speaks loudly, that he speaks clearly. Maybe my voice is not coming out, wonders Printz, perhaps I swallow my voice and it travels downward, into my stomach? That is why he asks Rikard: *What did I just say? Repeat what I just said.*

I need the toilet, says Rikard. *Cremations are wonderful in Bali, that's what you said.*

Rikard is an old fox, a wily old fox. Now he is a bit mournful, momentarily mournful, yes, he is mournful as he walks along this mountain where they should never have come. Ernestina has gone, yes, but what is Printz thinking, what? Why he, Rikard, knows all there is to know about Bali, he knows it all. He knows about the ducks and the temples and the cremations. They sent Printz there on his instruction, he told them Printz is reliable, he told them, *don't worry, it's all under control.* What is this Printz thinking, what? In Denpasar he sells his dinner suit, his special one, white like Suharto's, he sells his official car and hands money to the poor. In Bali there are a lot of poor people. They find him on the beach in the moonlight building sand replicas of Balinese temples and saying *leave me alone, I'm a sculptor, I'm a sculptor.* So he gives the order, Rikard gives the order that Printz Dvorsky be sent a letter *thank you, you will receive a pension,* he gives the order that he should be moved, he says *make sure it is humane.* Rikard knows that Printz ate bebek betutu in Bali at a dinner at Suharto's and that he lost state papers.

In Bali there's a temple, it's an old temple, nine centuries old, high on Mount Agung and it is called Mother Temple. That is what Printz says. As he talks, Printz hears a fairy tale and becomes emotional. Printz is glad that Tina is not lying in a dovecote because dovecotes are for doves to lay their eggs in and coo. Printz does not like doves.

You talk too much, Pupi, says Rikard. Rikard is anxious, he is not very anxious. Just a little.

Everything is cheerful in Bali. There's a lot of color. Don't call me Pupi. That is what Printz says.

Rikard and Printz go back to the hotel as Rikard needs the toilet and because the mountain night is falling and because they both want a bowl of soup. It is deserted.

Printz sometimes has explosions in his head. They are small explosions that do not hurt. When they come, those little explosions sparkle and then Printz becomes Pupi. It is like a light bulb shattering, like an idea shattering. One could say, it is like a little soap bubble bursting, but people often say that. Those explosions are like a soft "p" in Pupi's head, like a soft "p" crackling and emitting images that sparkle. Then Pupi blinks. Pupi blinks because tiny stories crackle in his head. Like now, as he and Rikard are making their way back to the hotel.

---------------------✂----------------------

Knut Andersen finds a solution for pigeons. Knut Andersen has a double-barrelled shotgun and he shoots pigeons. He lives on the main square in Oslo, far to the north and he is old. One day he kills 2001 pigeons; he paints 1900 pigeons yellow, 100 in other colors of the rainbow and just one white. The white pigeon is supposed to be the king. Knut Andersen stretches a wire across the central square in Oslo a hundred meters from the ground and hangs the dead stuffed painted pigeons from it, saying: *It's an installation for the new millennium.* There are a lot of feathers around Knut Andersen. He is like something from a dream, soft and elusive.

Knut Andersen has a plastic shopping bag like all homeless people. All his property is in his bag. He fills his bag with the remaining dead pigeons. *I'll make pie from my mother's recipe,* he says. Maybe Knut Andersen is Christian's brother, the one who writes fairy tales?

---------------------✂----------------------

In the hotel room the air is damp because the radiators are hissing. In the hotel room Printz decides: *I'll have body piercings done* and Rikard Dvorsky says: *We're leaving tomorrow.*

The key won't go into the lock. Neither Rikard's nor Printz's. The door opposite them in the corridor opens, it is a high door, thick and lacquered, oak. It is an elegant building, all the doors are polished and decorated with small shiny brass plates with famous names on them, locally famous, not globally. The door opposite opens and out comes the family of Herzog Dvorsky, in high spirits. The Rottweiler comes out too, also in high spirits for no reason. In the corridor, in part of the corridor, in the narrow space between the two doors on which is written Dvorsky and then Dvorsky again, there is a crowd. There is no one in the rest of the corridor; in the rest of the building silence reigns. The family of Herzog Dvorsky sings a little song of welcome to Rikard and Printz and it echoes. Everyone hops about. Including the dog. You can make out the words *welcome home, welcome home,* the tune is unfamiliar, a combination of occasional songs, an improvisation. The gay mood is also an improvisation, Printz realizes at once. Otherwise, in the Dvorsky family English is spoken as a matter of course. So *welcome home, welcome home* sounds quite natural.

Herzog says: M*atilda will explain everything.* That is what he says, because Herzog is not a brave man, they all know. Herzog too. Matilda is wearing a dress of Tina's, barely altered, blue, with little white flowers, a day dress, not a stage one.

We've altered the flat, says Matilda. She says it cheerfully.

Printz sees—Matilda's lips are pursed as she acts cheerfully so he does not want to look at her, he just turns his key between his fingers.

Herzog unlocks the door, he has a new key for the altered flat, a valid key. The dog barks. The children rush to the food, the table is full of food.

----------------------✂------------------------

Five hundred pickled cabbage rolls and two hundred people to celebrate Herzog's birth.

Five hundred pickled cabbages and two hundred people, repeats Aunty Hilda for days, so does Rikard, the rooms stink of sauerkraut and it is very crowded. Ernestina sings and cleans silver salvers. Then the festive evening arrives, the cabbages are on the table, the table is covered in cabbages, the drawing room is full of people. Printz does not know what to do with himself. *Where's Maristella?* he asks. No one hears. Printz is little and the guests are big and Printz looks at them from below.

I need to go, he says.

No one hears, the din is terrific. Printz shifts from one foot to the other and repeats *I need to go* and *where is Maristella?*

Herzog is very small. Herzog sleeps in a little cot upstairs and does not know that his birth is being celebrated in the drawing room, he does not know. The little cot upstairs has been placed next to Ernestina's big bed in which Rikard also sleeps. Printz's bed is not in that room.

Printz goes upstairs, into the room in which Herzog is sleeping in a small cot with rails. Printz is four years old. When he is asked *how old are you?* he says *eight.* Printz knows that he is four but he likes being eight because people keep asking him *how old are you, Pupi?* Printz does not like being called Pupi, he does not like being asked how old he is, he does not like being asked *what's your brother's name?* and people ask that even when they know what his brother's name is. *What's your brother's name,* they ask, and they know. Printz does not like that.

Printz takes off his trousers, squats and shits in the middle of the room.

A big turd, he says. *Good Pupi.*

Printz takes his turd and carries it to little Herzog who is sleeping: *Here you are, eat it.*

Herzog's face is covered in Printz's shit. Herzog wakes up and shrieks. Printz wipes his hands on the wall above Herzog's head and goes down to the kitchen. Some women are milling about the kitchen, his grandmother and Aunty Hilda. Printz says:

Aunty Hilda, Herzog's eating Pupi's poo-poo.

---------------------------------✂----------------------------

Where are the rooms? asks Rikard.

Rikard is standing beside the table of food and turning around on his axis. *Where are my rooms?*

(Printz's camp bed is folded up and put away under the window which, like the one in the kitchen, looks out at the street light.)

The dining room is a dark room. You cannot see anything out of it, just the other residents' old balconies. Those balconies are used for storing rubbish and broken washing machines and burned out cookers. They are balconies for rubbish, and high above them peers the framed sky. It is now like a room for dying in.

Where there had been double doors leading into the drawing room and then from the drawing room into the library, through which light came from the city, and noise, there is a wall, a new wall. The wall is pink. On it hangs the young Ernestina in a frame (oil on canvas), also in pink tones. Ernestina smiles even though she is dead.

Behind the wall is Herzog's extended flat. Herzog has extended his flat by adding Rikard's drawing room and Rikard's library. It is clear to everyone. Including Rikard. That is why it is quite stupid that Rikard is asking *where are my rooms*. What can you do? People ask stupid things.

Printz sings:

Everyone looks at Printz while he is singing. As he sings, Printz smiles a little. Just a little.

Printz appears delighted but he is not. He is about to start speaking, he knows that, senses it. Words rise in his throat as though he was going to vomit. They will look at him, all of them including Rikard and the Rottweiler, and Herzog will say: *cut the crap, Pupi.* Nevertheless, Printz says:

Once a learned man brought Diogenes into a richly furnished house and told him: "On no account spit on the floor." Diogenes had a sudden urge to cough and, not having anywhere to put the phlegm, he hawked it up and spat it into the man's face. Then he exclaimed enthusiastically: "Your snout is the only place dirty enough for expectoration." That was good, thinks Printz, satisfied with his little story. That is what he concluded.

Where am I going to sleep? asks Rikard.

Oh, Matilda scampers in Ernestina's blue and white silk dress so the dress flutters, *Oh, Daddy, your bedroom is wonderful!* Matilda calls Rikard Daddy because she thinks it sounds cheerful and warm. She thinks it is intimate and elegant.

How do I get to my bedroom, asks Rikard, *now you've walled me in?*

Through the toilet, says Matilda. When she says "through the toilet," it does not occur to her to repeat "Daddy."

They all, six of them plus the dog, march off through the bathroom to Rikard's bedroom, the one with the little white dressing table, white wardrobes and crystal mirrors. They all go to see how wonderful Rikard's bedroom is.

Where's my bed? asks Rikard. He asks because the large bed in which Ernestina lay dying is no longer in the room. In the room there is just a small bed, a narrow bed, cut in half. In the room there is in fact half a bed. It is now an incomplete bed. Naturally, the crystal mirror is not there, what would Rikard want with a mirror, especially a crystal one? If he really wants to look at his old face, there is a shaving mirror in the bathroom.

Printz senses an explosion in the making in his head. He hears it approaching, hears it ticking like a primed bomb, but a small one. This time it will be a quiet crack, not dangerous, Printz knows. He always knows. That is why he is calm.

-------------------------✂-------------------------

In the middle of the renovated room lies Rikard, in the shape of a carpet, flat and downtrodden. It is a shabby, thin carpet but still, it is Rikard Dvorsky. Over the carpet tread people from Rikard's past, unknown people walk up and down, they do not speak, they just tread, the carpet-Rikard is relaxed, you can see—he feels nothing. Rikard's eyes are open because he is watching the procession from his past. There is no Ernestina. All at once Rikard begins to grow: from a two-dimensional carpet he is transformed into a three-dimensional carpet that rises like dough. Rikard grows to five centimeters thick, then suddenly stops growing, just stops. Like a lift that shudders to a halt. Rikard is now a fairly thick carpet of lively colors. It could be a Tabriz, definitely not a Bokhara, because they are red and Rikard is bluish. He is bluish all over. And soft. It is a pleasure to walk on him. *It hurts,* whispers Rikard. It is unclear whether Rikard is weeping or just moaning. Seen from above, one cannot see whether Rikard is weeping, for even if he was, his tears would have nowhere to flow. Only possibly back into the woollen material with a lot of knots. It is an expensive carpet.

---------------------✂--------------------

Beside the window of Rikard's emptied bedroom is the pink armchair. Through the window the street can be seen. Light comes through the window. Rikard can now sit for hours in the pink armchair, watching life go by.

I'll write to Maristella, tonight, he says. *Maybe she will help.* No one hears because there is no one there. Printz is in the kitchen drinking milk. Standing up.

There are days when Pupi changes into a fly. That happens when someone makes him angry. Then he buzzes, buzzes, all around, mainly high up, near the ceiling. When he gets tired, he knocks into the wall and that is how he calms down. Now he is very upset (or angry), so the Pupi-fly bangs his head against the wall several times. Flies have small heads so that banging against a wall is invisible to humans. So no one knows anything about it. Only Pupi knows but he keeps that secret to himself. When it happens, Pupi shakes his head as though he cannot see properly, as though he wants to sharpen the image, but he just says *my vision is blurry.*

Sometimes Pupi dreams that he is walking along broad avenues along which human heads roll, human heads with faces he knows. Then Pupi plays football with those human heads, kicks them, but sometimes he bowls with them. Pupi loves bowling. The heads fall apart, their teeth fall out and they get bloody.

Pupi also often goes to war. That gives him inner satisfaction, that going off to battle sometimes across soft borders, sometimes impenetrable ones. Pupi no longer knows whether he is going to help the people from Vukovar or the ones from Sarajevo, he does not know. But in this war he becomes a hero and is proud of himself. He saves people, takes them out of their hiding places, bandages their wounds, tells the children stories. Sometimes he sees fields of unscythed wheat, sometimes streets flooded with plastic bags in which frozen feces are thawing, human. He listens to people saying *This is a terrible war, it is a small war and it will soon be over* so Pupi is calm, he knows that he will survive. But still, in this war there are dead people, too many dead people. In this war there is an invalid whom Pupi regularly visits. He is a special invalid, Pupi thinks. One of his legs is missing, he has only a stump that keeps bleeding, that will not heal and that is why the stump is wrapped in bandages. That invalid often hops along after Pupi, in fact he accompanies him. Sometimes, the invalid smiles at Pupi and then Pupi is pleased. *It suggests that the end is near,* Pupi believes, *when the invalid smiles at me.* Sometimes, the invalid suddenly starts to lose weight, melts, disappears. He becomes a skeleton. As he disappears, he looks more and more like Pupi and in the end he becomes him, Pupi. His head turns into a skull that grimaces. That frightens Pupi, it frightens him a lot and then the picture shatters. All that remains are clouds of blue steam.

---------------------✂-----------------------

No way, as long as Ernestina is ill, says Rikard Dvorsky. He says it sternly but quietly, Rikard Dvorsky is good at that.

Printz pays for a two-day tourist trip to Budapest and sets off, with no suitcase. On Margitsziget island, on the east side, by the ruins of a Dominican convent, he waits for seven hours, until it gets dark, he pees three times, kills mosquitoes and wanders up and down. For four hours the rain pours in torrents, it makes transparent curtains that fall from the sky like a wet spider's web through which the greenery of Margitsziget is broken up. *I'd like to go into that greenery,* says Printz, *I'd like to go in to get lost, that green is like the green used by the painter Safet Zec.* His contact does not come. In the hotel a small man in black patent winklepickers is waiting for him.

The small man says: *It's pouring and Budapest is deep green.*

Printz asks: *Are you a poet?*

The secret agent smiles mysteriously, so it seems to Printz.

Your contact is dead. Your contact has been murdered or he may have committed suicide. That is what the small man in the brown leather jacket says.

What do I do now? asks Printz.

Nothing. You won't do anything. You won't cross over. You'll go back. That's that. There's a war on. We're being attacked and we're defending ourselves. People are dying, there are ruins. That is what the man from the neighboring country says. Then he leaves.

Printz's head is swimming. Printz's head is full of small corpses floating, small pink corpses, children. Over them, like open umbrellas float lovely young women, very white. Also dead, completely dead. *Oh, you won't be able to protect them, you won't be able to protect your little pink children, no,* shouts Printz. *The world is full of twins who carry in their insides the embryos of their brothers and sisters, rotten, black and brown. Petrified.* Printz shouts, his eye sockets are drumming, but no one hears that because Printz is shouting inwardly and from the outside he is just looking at the hotel porter. The small man from the next-door country, the country in which he, Printz, was born, is no longer there. In his place there is a hole in the air.

Printz asks the porter, the hotel porter, in a blue and gold uniform, he asks him: *Where is the grave of Ignác Semmelweis?* Printz wants to go to the grave of Ignác Semmelweis immediately, that is why he asks the porter *where is the grave of Ignác Semmelweis?,* that is why. The porter is polite, porters do not ask many questions, it is generally the guests who ask, porters reply. This blue and yellow porter is not remotely interested in why someone would want to visit the grave of Ignác Semmelweis, that is quite clear to Printz. It is also clear that porters are not obliged to know anything about Ignác Semmelweis, even if they are Hungarian porters, Budapest porters. What do porters need Ignác Semmelweis for, what?

Take a taxi, says the porter. *The cemetery is called Kerepesi.*

Printz wants to see the monument to Ignác Semmelweis, because with the departure of the small secret agent from the next-door country, Printz is abruptly overwhelmed by sadness for Ignác Semmelweis. He suddenly feels terribly sad. Oh, what dreadful injustice was done to Ignác Semmelweis, dreadful. Printz is not sure whether what is growing in him is sadness or perhaps disquiet, he is not sure. When one goes on a trip to Budapest as a tourist, it is logical to visit Kerepesi cemetery, is it not? Many well known people lie in Kerepesi cemetery. Besides, when he goes on tourist excursions Printz wants to see as much as possible because you never know whether there will be another tourist trip, specifically a tourist trip. You never know. Particularly not now, when his connection has failed, when the man who was to take him across is dead, killed, has committed suicide. Who knows.

If Ignác Semmelweis had not been born, perhaps neither would he, Printz, have been born. Perhaps Ernestina would have died of sepsis because her baby might have been delivered by a doctor, or even a student, who had just dissected a corpse and had not washed his hands. Oh, there is something wrong with Printz's head. In his head time melts, loses its outlines, disperses into blots. That happens to Printz, yes, so he does not know which century he is in, or where he is.

Get a grip, Pupi. Ignác Semmelweis died in 1865.

There is no Ignác Semmelweis at the Kerepesi cemetery. There is just a monument, and beneath it—nothing. The monument to Ignác Semmelweis slants toward the ground like an ornament, a large ornament of yellowed stone, with soft clumps of moss, because Ignác Semmelweis died long ago, and the Kerepesi cemetery is damp, that is why there is moss. Ignác Semmelweis was burned and poured into an urn, and the urn is kept in a glass case in the Medical History Museum, but Printz does not want to go to the Medical History Museum in Budapest, he wants to go to Kerepesi cemetery.

Plot 34/2, says the official at the information office. Yes, Kerepesi cemetery has an information office because a lot of tourists visit Budapest, tourists like going to cemeteries, so the cemeteries make sure the tourists do not roam pointlessly around the cemetery. Printz concludes that it is after all stupid to go to foreign cemeteries, generally there is no close relative or friend in foreign cemeteries. What do tourists need that for? What does he need that for? He would be better off eating cakes. Oh, yes, cakes in

Budapest! As soon as he has visited Ignác, he will go for some cakes, for sure.

Hold on, Pupi, think for a minute. It's getting dark, the cemetery gate is closing.

From plot 34/2 Printz is observed by two lions' heads. And he, Printz, observes them.

They are fine stone lions, strong lions, benign. Ignác Semmelweis died on August 13, 1865 in Vienna, that is what it says on the monument and in fact he died in the National Institute for the Mentally Ill in Döbling, aged forty-seven, he was a doctor and— mad, they said. Mad? Vienna would not have him. Vienna told him, *Go away, go back where you came from, go back to your Budapest.* Ignác Semmelweis goes back to his Budapest and in his Budapest he helps women give birth, they do not die of pyemia but stay alive, they do not die of puerperal fever like all those women giving birth in Vienna, because Ignác Semmelweis washes his hands in chlorinated water and in Budapest it is no longer permitted to dissect bodies and then attend births with unwashed hands. Why the sick Ignác Semmelweis returns to Vienna, or rather to Döbling, is not known, perhaps he is taken by force to that National Institute for the Mentally Ill. Is there no hospital for the mind in Budapest at that time? I cannot go back to the country where I was born, the people in whose country I stayed to live are killing people in the country where I was born, my connection is no more, I am not a doctor and the times are different, completely different. If Ernestina had given birth in Vienna at the time when they drove Doctor Ignác Semmelweis out of Vienna, she would have died of sepsis, she could most certainly have died and I would have been born blue and dead.

You were born blue, Pupi.

I wasn't.

Look at the different ways his name is spelled, the name

Semmelweis: it is written Ignaz Philipp and Ignác Fülöp. While the surname Semmelweis is not touched. *Was he a Jew? Maybe he was a Jew.*

Don't talk rubbish, Pupi. Keep walking.

Printz walks on and breathes deeply. It is an extensive cemetery, Kerepesi cemetery, there is lots of greenery. Printz stops at plot 28, because it is near plot 34/2 where the monument to Ignác Semmelweis is. On plot 28 there is an enormous statue, completely white, stone-white, frightening.

The four horsemen of the apocalypse, all four of them in stone, petrified, says Printz, looking.

In plot 28, under the white horsemen of the apocalypse, lies József Attila. Printz does not know whether to be glad that he has met another acquaintance or sorrowful because of the destiny of the young poet, son of a washerwoman and secret member of the secret Communist Party. József Attila was an impoverished child, an impoverished student, an impoverished poet, terribly impoverished. Had he lived in his day, Printz would have helped him, for certain. He would have brought him food, offered him his bed. From his seventh year, József Attila did all kinds of jobs, that was when his father left, abandoning him and his mother, then József Attila was moved from one family to another, and none of them was kind to him, and while he was still small, only nine, he tried to kill himself. Then his mother died although he, József Attila, was still not quite grown, he was only fourteen, in fact he was small and unprotected, his mother, the washerwoman, died, exhausted, worn out, full of wrinkles and done in, and József Attila was left alone. He spent some twenty years figuring out how to kill himself and in the end, of course, he killed himself. This time successfully, forever, but Printz did not know how. He would have to research it. As soon as he gets home, Printz will try to discover how József Attila killed himself: Atilla, a brilliant student, József Attila, a poet whose poems no one read at the time. Later, much later, some people decided to remember József Attila and make him famous, only that was no use to him because he had been dead for a long time already, as indeed had Ignác Semmelweis. Ignác Semmelweis is often mentioned today as well, people write novels and plays about him. Unhappy men, unlucky, both of them. Printz bends down toward the gravestone and reads: József Attila, 1905–1937.

Printz stops at plot 26 and, look, he's smiling! On plot 26 stands the enormous statue of a man in a long white shirt, open. The shirt looks as though it is made of flour, soft. The shirt flutters although everything on Kerepesi cemetery is still. Even the birds.

There don't seem to be any birds.

Yes, there do not seem to be any birds, where are the birds?

The statue is gazing at the sky. Who is it?

Oh, Emil Gerbeaud! says Printz. Printz runs his hand over the lower part of the statue because it is tall, twice as tall as Printz, perhaps three times, and that cheerful statue is so white, so clean, one really could say it is a cheerful statue, yes, then, waving to Mr. Gerbeaud, he sets off toward the exit with a brisk step, which is unusual for Printz in recent times, any kind of physical speed.

Vörösmarty téri—Gerbeaud, says Printz to the taxi driver, who says *ooh la la!* as though he is from Paris.

Dobos torte? No. All credit to Mr. József Dobos, the owner of a delicatessen and cake shop, successful writer of some fifteen cookbooks in German. Kugler torte with walnuts, filled with thick chocolate cream and scattered with little chocolate flakes. No, as early as 1870, Mr. Kugler opened a shop in the heart of old Budapest and exclaimed *these are mignons, ladies and gentlemen, try my mignons.* When Gerbeaud bought Kugler's shop there was a real craze for sweet things in Budapest. Budapest licked its fingers. Mignons? It could not be said that Printz adored mignons, if he ever had to choose, then no, the mignons fail. Sacher? Franz Sacher, former kitchen dogsbody and dishwasher at Count Metternich's, who thanks to the head chef's day off had the opportunity to prepare a feast for his boss and guests and to create a culinary hit. But that had happened in Vienna, long ago, in Vienna today the former kitchen boy has rich and famous descendants, owners of the famous Hotel Sacher, immediately behind the building of the Opera at 4 Philharmonikerstrasse, where that Jewish tart Charlotte Rampling known as Lucia takes part in sadomasochistic sessions with the night porter Dirk Bogarde, the former SS member Max. Sacher torte, yes, Printz adores Sacher torte, especially with local apricot jam that merges miraculously with the thick chocolate covering. With which one drinks cold milk, a liter, two. No, that is Vienna, and Printz is in Budapest. Sacher torte, no.

Kossuth's little horns of whipped egg-white with ground walnuts? That is Lajos Kossuth, the fighter for national independence, persecuted and imprisoned. Why did he get little horns and not some thick cake soaked in rum, filled with chopped candied fruit, covered in cream, why not something like that? He got little meringues, light as foam, cheerful, mischievous little white half-moons. Printz does not eat those little frothy creations, ever.

Garibaldi cake? Garibaldi, the national fighter who dreamed of a united Italy. In history there are quite a few national fighters and uniters. People dream stupidities. There were Hungarians in Garibaldi's army, only it is not known whether they had the same dream as Garibaldi. Maybe they did not care, there are also those who do not dream about unification but about love. They are more sexual types, less warlike. Oh, it is a long time since Printz has been with a woman, he will have to do something about it, he will have to. Small animals were abandoning him, he was thinking about cakes, that was a good sign. In Hungary today people eat Garibaldi squares in memory and honor of the Hungarian soldiers who were killed. That must be why. Garibaldi squares are tasty. Covered in jam and sprinkled with almonds and walnuts, covered with egg-white beaten with sugar then baked. Printz does not like baked egg-white, that is why he will not eat Garibaldi squares in Budapest, no. Beaten and baked egg-white gives cakes a flutteriness, a deceptive lightness which does not appeal to Printz. Printz likes rich cakes, moist, he does not like hiccuping while he is eating cakes. Printz normally eats quickly and now he is thirsty.

Esterházy torte? Baked apples à la Josephine?

The patisserie is elegant. Oh, that Gerbeaud, what a gourmet! No one knows why he left his native Switzerland, but he did, people leave their home countries, it happens all the time. There are people who never leave the country in which they were born, they refuse to. They think it is not okay, it's like leaving your mother. Printz does not agree with that way of thinking. Printz thinks that you must leave your mother, especially if your mother is called Ernestina. When he left Switzerland, Gerbeaud invented a magical sweet, filled with cognac, with a firm dark red morello cherry floating in it, drunk with pleasure. That was how Gerbeaud compensated for the loss of his homeland and his mother. And the loss of his large Swiss chocolate factory. Sweets compensate for various losses, that is a well known fact. After Germany, France and England, Gerbeaud settled in Hungary and in Budapest created his Gerbeaud torte. As yet another compensation. That compensation brought him fame. And fortune. Perhaps Printz would be able to invent something, something by way of compensation. Printz would like to succeed in something. He had thought of going to his homeland, to his fatherland and his motherland to help save the wounded, Printz liked helping. He had wanted to go to where he was born, but it turned out badly. That contact should not have died just then, he could have died later, once he had got him, Printz, across. Now that had failed. But Ernestina refused to die.

In the Gerbeaud cake shop the walls were covered in silk wallpaper, the little tables were made of marble, the lights crystal. In the Gerbeaud everything around hummed with an elegance that suited Printz, Printz liked elegance, it was an elegance from another age, past. The air smelled of chocolate, Printz found himself in chocolate nirvana and he thought that he was going to faint.

I'm going to faint, he said. To himself. To the waitress he said: *Four slices of Gerbeaud torte and three glasses of cold milk.* His hands lay on the marble surface of the marble Kaffeetisch. *I've got nice hands,* he said, also to himself. *And I'm tired.*

Printz left Budapest. The tourists sang. The tourists were also leaving Budapest, they were returning to the town on the confluence of two polluted rivers, returning from their excursion, from their shopping trip. They were happy, you could see, because they were singing. Budapest is a beautiful city. Printz heard shells falling over there (Vukovar?), he saw bombers flying over there, they seemed close, they were not going far, the woman beside him in the bus said, *The Hungarians have excellent cheeses and cheap salami, no worse than what they produce in the breakaway republics.*

When Printz got home, Rikard repeated: *Don't be an idiot, you can't leave, we can't leave Ernestina.*

Herzog would not dream of going secretly to where there was a war. Herzog would not dream of going to any battlefield, because Herzog did not know how to hold a gun, because he had dodged the army when it was still peacetime and because he did not want to leave his Rottweiler. *I'd die without my Rottweiler,* that is what he said. Herzog was fat and said nothing. He invited guests for a beer and nibbles. Matilda said: *My Herzog is a man of morals, he does not get involved.*

That was 1991. Or 1992? It took Ernestina another three years to die. Perhaps more? Then it was too late.

I'm stuck now, said Printz.

---------------------------✂----------------------------

Printz drinks his milk and goes to the bathroom. He picks up some nail scissors and starts making holes in his body, all over his thighs and belly, on his shoulders, behind, as far down as he can reach. He uses the little scissors to perforate and twist as though his body was a field, as though he was preparing a large, quiet expanse of land for cultivation, for seeds. Blood pours out of the little craters, of course. Printz watches. *I'll keep piercing until milk starts pouring out of me instead of blood,* he says. *I'm full of milk. I drink too much milk.* Then Printz goes into Rikard Dvorsky's bedroom and says: *Don't worry, I'll make dinner.*

Rikard Dvorsky does not look around, he sits motionless in the pink armchair, looking out of the window. Printz repeats *don't worry, it'll be all right,* but Rikard Dvorsky whispers: *I think I'm going to die.* And dies.

Rikard Dvorsky is dead, Printz announces to the dirty window and goes on looking into the urban distance.

Printz has no idea what to do.

I'll sell my microscope, it's an expensive microscope and valuable.

We need to get money together for another cremation.

I'll sell these pictures on the walls.

Printz gets drunk. Printz drinks that day and the next. He drinks a lot and for a long time. Printz is first half-conscious, then unconscious. It is white wine, bad wine, that Printz drinks. Then he vomits.

The formalities of the cremation of Rikard Dvorsky are carried out by Herzog, dedicatedly and pedantically. The cremation leaves no impression on Printz.

It's all old hat, we've been there before, concludes Printz.

The urn is placed in the depot, right next to Ernestina. Now both urns are waiting. Waiting to go to their hometowns, to a different country.

Small animals move into Printz's head. He looks after his little animals; feeds them and settles them to sleep. Sometimes they are alive and they move, sometimes they are like porcelain figures and stand still, stiff.

Like me. I sometimes stiffen on purpose.

All Printz's little animals are the same size regardless of what kind they are. So there is a grotesque disharmony in Printz's head.

What disharmony? There's no disharmony.

Cats, small cats, big as dogs, small dogs. Small rhinos, as small as small birds, like snakes, lions, bugs.

Bugs? What bugs?

Cicadas.

Don't mention cicadas. Cicadas are a special kind of bug. They eat roots. For three, sometimes four years, they live under ground and travel toward the light. When they catch sight of the sun, cicadas sing, fall in love and die.

The ancient Greeks adored cicadas. They kept them in little cages.

The Romans did not adore cicadas. The Romans were irritated by cicadas. They killed them and fed them to ants.

Printz is still sleeping on the narrow camp bed next to the dining table. He does not want to lie in the Dvorskys' halved marital bed, which is empty now that Rikard has gone too. Printz reads and visits exhibitions. He looks for Maristella.

Maristella has gone. Maristella is now in a different country. Printz does not wish to know that.

Printz changes his clothes increasingly rarely. Printz has a lot of holes on his body. When the old holes heal, he makes new ones with scissors. He is waiting for milk to come out of him.

Leave me alone. Leave me.

He is full of craters, he is scabby.

He studies the year of his birth.

It was not a good year to be born, no.

It was 1946.

It was the year Charlotte Rampling was born, she has small tits and yellow eyes like a cobra, dangerous eyes. She was born at the same time as me.

Printz keeps company with newspaper sellers because he has no friends anymore, some have died, some have got lost, some have left, their contacts were not killed, and he had washed Ernestina and then walked with Rikard on a small wet mountain, on a hill, in fact. In the next-door country, Maristella is preparing an exhibition to which Printz will go, certainly, he will try. Over the counter, Printz tells the women selling newspapers, *I've brought you a cup of coffee and a silk dress, for the stage.* Then he hands the items to them. The newspaper sellers smile and take them, because newspaper sellers like it when clothes shimmer. Most of all they like clothes with sequins and blouses shot through with silver and gold thread, but there are no more of those, Printz has given them all away. The shop assistants are not interested in Rikard's clothes, at night Printz had put Rikard's suits beside the trash can, one by one, then from the window he watched who took what. When he hands the shop assistants his small gifts (Ernestina's actually), Printz says *I haven't got any cigarettes* and they give him some. Sometimes Printz brings the shop assistants a crystal glass, or rather two, for what would they do with one. He brings Ernestina's jewelry, the remains of Ernestina's jewelry, most of it was taken by Herzog and Matilda. Printz has two such shop assistants, in case of need. The assistants love Printz. Printz tells them stories that they do not entirely understand but which sound both nice and terrible so they are a bit afraid. The assistants like that, that ticklish secret fear because they know it is harmless, because they are behind the counter, protected.

In the elegant Vienna hotel, very elegant, the most elegant Vienna hotel, called Sacher, in which everything is chocolate brown like Sacher torte and stuffy in the style of the Habsburgs, Charlotte Rampling meets the torturer of her life, Dirk Bogarde, who is not called Dirk but Maximilian like that unfortunate archduke and admiral of the Austrian navy, later emperor of Mexico, whom Juarez in the town of Querétaro forces to surrender and in 1867 has him court-martialled, then he is condemned to death and shot. But that, such a tragic death does not happen to this Max, no. Charlotte is called Lucia, because, given that this is 1957 and in real life Charlotte Rampling is only eleven and at eleven there is no way that she would do everything that Lucia does with Maximilian in room 421. The Sacher Hotel is just opposite the Opera House at 4 Philharmonikerstrasse. That is why both of them, both Charlotte Rampling and Dirk Bogarde have different names and both of them live lives that are not their own, but pretend that they are, convincingly, pretty convincingly, yes.

I was in Vienna, officially and secretly, not in the Sacher Hotel but the Kummer Hotel, which is at 71a Mariahilfer Strasse and is less elegant than the Sacher Hotel although it is still fairly elegant. This is a digression.

Never mind, says the shop assistant benignly, as though wanting to comfort Printz.

Eleven years later, Max and Lucia meet by chance in the Vienna Sacher Hotel because there is peace in the world then. It's a story like a fairy tale, completely made up and full of subdued light. Max is the night porter and Lucia is classy, she has a rich husband with the English name Atherton and she travels everywhere with him. Max and Lucia meet and immediately remember everything that happened in the concentration camp all that time ago, when Max was an SS officer and Lucia a Jewess. In the camp Lucia sang and danced and Max fucked and tortured her, then she whipped him because Max was a complex personality who made love with both sexes, receiving and inflicting pain. And now, in Vienna, in the Sacher Hotel, they remember all that with such nostalgia that they want to repeat everything that happened then, they want to do it again, to do more, this time perhaps a bit more cruelly, a bit more terribly, aware that there are no great dangers anymore because the world is at peace. There are no more terrible gifts reminiscent of the story of Salome and John the Baptist. None. And so, Lucia and Max put on little dislocated performances in peacetime Vienna, which arouse them sexually because Lucia is rich and free while Max is nobody, in fact an ordinary night porter even if in a deluxe category hotel.

Who is Salome? asks the shop assistant.

Sometimes stories get mixed up in Printz's head, some characters enter them and others depart. Dirk Bogarde is not Maximilian anymore, but Herman who in reality is called Dragoš. The shop assistants listen anyway, they click their tongues and ask: *then what happened?*

Printz says: *Then Herman coaxes Lucia to stay in Vienna forever, to stay with him so that they can spend the rest of their lives whipping each other, wrapped in chains and black leather straps. "I'll show you the most beautiful city in the world, my world," says Herman. "I'll show you the last remnants of the Holy Roman Empire, the last dream of the greatness of a united Europe. I'll take you to the Prater, from high up we will watch the people below and see what only eagles see. That is the secret of contempt. In the evening, we'll drink an aperitif in the Loosbar and then go to dinner in the Drei Hacken. I'll take you to the Spanish Riding School and to lunch at the Opera."*

The Opera is opposite the Sacher Hotel, says Printz, then continues: *"We'll order music," Herman does not stop coaxing Lucia. "We'll*

order Lehar, I shall open my arms wide and say: C'est la vie! You'll meet
my friends from various phases of my life. They drink good wines from
private vineyards and still live in a youthful K und K style. Vienna
is for those who long for greatness, and that is us, Lucia, you and I."

Lucia looks at Herman and is not certain whether that is exactly
what she wants, although she does know that she will not agree to
absolute incarceration in room 421 of the Sacher Hotel, no way.

"We shall protect Vienna from the influx of foreigners and thus expi-
ate our sins. The infection of the degenerate Jewish plague is spreading
through the world, my dear Lucia," says Herman, then he tears his shirt
open and orders: "Whip me!"

1946 was the year Amanda Lear was born, and Fassbinder. Aleks-
andr Gorshkov, the figure skater, was born. Printz enters all this
into the remaining pages of the plucked black notebook. These
are his topics for his new friends. He collects subjects, he collects
little stories in exchange for free newspapers, free cigarettes, for
the occasional grandchild. He knows the free gifts will soon stop.

Liza Minnelli was born, Alexander Shaparenko (USSR, Olympic
gold for kayak, 1972), the Mongolian wrestler Bakhaavaa Buidda was
born.

Printz makes a list of the dead and executed in 1946. That year,
1946, there were a lot of executions. On his list there are few actors
or singers, few researchers or sportsmen, but a lot of previously
dangerous people. On the list are also those whom Printz loves,
and he makes up tender stories about them, touching and filmic,
so that the newspaper sellers shed tears.

I like it when they cry, I like that.

Printz does not know why he is replacing one list, his parents',
that everyday, consumer one, with another, his own. He does not
know. On Printz's list from 1946 there are: Alfred Jodl, general,
hanged; Hermann Göring, Nazi, Reichsmarschall, poisoned himself with cyanide in prison; Wilhelm Frick, German war crimi-

nal, hanged; Arthur Seyss-Inquart, Austrian Chancellor in 1938, hanged; August Borms, Flemish collaborator, executed; Alfred Rosenberg, German war criminal, hanged; the Yugoslav general Dragoljub Draža Mihailović, collaborated with the Nazis, hanged; Fawzi Husseini, high Arab functionary for Palestine, killed; Clemens von Galen, Bishop of Münster, antifascist, died of natural causes (at 68); Ernst Kaltenbrunner, Austrian Nazi, hanged; Gertrude Stein, American-French poet and writer, died; Fritz Sauckel, German war criminal, hanged; H.G. Wells, writer, died (79); Ion Antonescu, Romanian fascist prime minister and dictator, killed; Joachim von Ribbentrop, German war criminal, hanged; Hans Frank, German war criminal, hanged; Julius Streicher, German leader, hanged; Wilhelm Keitel, German field-marshal, hanged.

What a year to be born! Terrible. The Spanish composer Manuel de Falla, famous for his composition *La vida breve*, died.

Printz notes that in 1946, the first auto-bank was established, in America of course; natural cloud was made into the first artificial snow, also in America; at the Paris fashion show, the first bikini was displayed. Those are cheerful details, oh yes. Printz's shop assistants will like that. The first electric blanket was produced, retailing at 39.50 US dollars. But Printz knows: when he was born, there were anti-Jewish demonstrations in Poland, 39 people died while he was being born; Churchill (in a manic phase) advocated the establishment of the United States of Europe, after the earthquake in Japan, there were 1086 dead, while he, Printz, was being born. The Emperor Hirohito announced that he was not a god after all, Klement Gottwald became prime minister of Czechoslovakia. The United States condemned to death 58 guards from the Mauthausen camp, 46 SS officers from Dachau and detonated the first atomic bomb near Bikini, having previously dropped one on the atoll itself. Yugoslavia adopted a new constitution and became a federal republic, the USA recognized Tito's Yugoslavia while

Churchill (in a depressive phase) gave his famous speech about the Iron Curtain. For the New Year festivities, December 28, 1946, Rikard purchased, in the co-operative store, biscuits, chocolate and cheese, figs, 5 Unra packets and sweets for 873 dinars. Printz refuses to suckle. That is how 1946 ends.

It does not end, says Printz.

Printz paces round the stump of Rikard's flat, he has no idea what to do with himself. He circles around the table. Perhaps he is thinking. Two months have passed since his father's death. Then he asks:

W*hat are the rhinos doing?* and goes out.

There are no rhinos, it is cold.

Naturally, the zoo is deserted and white. Somehow transparent.

Printz goes to his secret lair, behind the west wall of the fortress, he bends down and peers in.

It's dry inside.

Then he goes in and sits amongst the trash. It's not bad, thinks Printz, it's dry. *It's dry,* he says out loud. Then he goes home.

Herzog is waiting at the door. Matilda too. They are waiting together. The Rottweiler is not there, it is probably eating. They do not say *welcome home,* especially not Matilda. Matilda is wearing pink slippers which glisten because they are made of pink satin, with a pompom made of feathers, a feather-duster, on the front, also pink, and the feathers jiggle, and the front of the slipper is pointed, the slippers are pointed like the shoes of the secret police in postwar socialism. Printz thinks they are ugly slippers, especially those pink feathers.

You've got ugly slippers, he says.

Matilda has big feet. In these slippers she looks exactly like Cinderella's sister, that wicked sister who shoves her foot into the small glass shoe, which does not fit her, only because Matilda is fat and her foot is fleshy. How joyful glass shoes are! They are transparent, they do not carry secrets, they fit in your hand because they are usually small and delicate, those glass shoes, miniature shoes in fact, out of a fairy tale. A little inattention and they are gone. Glass shoes cannot be mended, when they break, that is it. How would it be if we were like that, made of glass, wonders Printz, how would it be then?

Glass?

Transparent. With colored glass organs, various colors, multi-colored inside. Yellow spleen, red heart, brown liver, nerves—violet, gray, white, thin threads that form a web that prevents one seeing into the depths. I'd like to be like that, made of glass. I would like to have been blown by a blower twisting me over white fire. That my history, the history of my birth was this: hot and soft to the point of incandescence while the blower forms me; I bend and curl, contracting, coming into being, dripping the occasional glass tear, in fact a tiny ball, yes, a tiny ball, balls that stiffen as they fall, set and clink. Oh, how I would love to drip, to cry like glass, oh. Blown glass dies in water and remains lovely forever, shaped, clean, odorless. In water it yelps, sizzles, and dies. Glass people, yes, with veins and arteries of little blue and red glass tubes, hollow, through which nothing flows, nothing at all. Because glass blood does not exist, let us not deceive ourselves.

Enough, Pupi! Stop it!

If we were able always to free ourselves by weeping from the misery that overcomes us, obscure illnesses and poetry would disappear. But some innate refusal, intensified by upbringing, or some defect in the functioning of our tear glands, condemns us to the torment of dry eyes.

Stop!

Consequently, we are all sick, each of us lacks a Sahara where we would be able to shout at the top of our voices, or the shores of a dark, savage sea, with whose crazed sobs we could merge our own, still more furious.

That's enough, Pupi! Listen to what they are saying, Pupi. Listen to what Herzog and Matilda have to say.

Printz does not like the story of Cinderella. He finds it a horrible story because it has too much tension, like *King Lear*, because those wicked sisters remind him of Herzog. That is why. Herzog is his brother, Printz's brother. But he likes the glass shoe. He likes that. It is a little fragile shoe. Lovely. Pupi likes that part of the story.

Herzog and Matilda are standing at the door, waiting.

When they catch sight of Printz, Herzog and Matilda do not say "oh daddy" because there is no daddy, daddy is standing on a shelf with Ernestina, in the depot, where it is cold, where a deathly, corpse-like coldness, unimaginable, reigns. That is why Herzog and Matilda do not smile, that is why, because neither Rikard nor Ernestina is here.

You've got ugly slippers, Printz says again. *And your name is ugly. You've got an ugly name, Matilda.*

Herzog says: *This is my flat now. Move out.*

Matilda says: *Yes, move out. We have to expand.*

Herzog adds: *Take what you need.*

Matilda adds: *Yes, take what you need.*

Printz says: *All right.*

Printz has a Samsonite briefcase, it is unbelievable how much it holds and it is easy to carry. Printz's Samsonite briefcase has a coded lock so no one can break into it. Apart from that, it is black, gray-black, anthracite. When Printz bought it (at Zurich airport on his way back from Oslo, 1987), anthracite was a fashionable color, and the salesgirl had told him: *Take this one, it projects power. You are a powerful man.* Nowadays, Samsonite luggage is produced in a lot of bright colors, but Printz's briefcase, black, never gets dirty.

This briefcase never gets dirty, says Printz.

Printz adores his *Encyclopædia Britannica* in 32 volumes. He bought it with a 20% discount for $796, when it normally cost $995. He gets all sorts of facts out of it, for Printz loves facts. Printz trusts facts, he believes in facts. Facts do not invent anything, facts do not deceive, as for example church facts deceive, faith facts, facts about God, which are not facts at all, but lies. Such facts irritate Printz because in recent years there have been a lot of them, more and more.

Faith facts get on my nerves, he says.

Printz reads and prepares to leave. He reads the *Encyclopædia Britannica* and tears out the pages he intends to take with him because 32 volumes will not fit into his black Samsonite briefcase. Printz also tears pages out of the books piled up in the corners, in the remaining corners of the amputated flat. (The room with shelves, the library, is in Herzog's part, partitioned off, but as soon as Printz leaves, that wall will come down and the flat will be spacious again.)

Yes, they will expand.

Printz buys fifty liters of milk. For a week he sits on the floor, in his pyjamas, reading. He chooses pages and puts them into his Samsonite briefcase, gray-black. He does not wash, he does not eat.

Where is your strength to refrain from the compulsion to breathe? Why should you continue to put up with the dense air that blocks your lungs and oppresses your body? How can you overcome those opaque hopes and petrified ideas now, when at one moment you imitate the solitude of stone, and the next you feel as rejected as spit stuck on the edge of the world? You are more distant from your own self than from any remote planet, and your senses, focused on graves, suspect that there is more life there than in the senses themselves ...

Printz reads all kinds of things like that. He enjoys them, those bitter lines, they give him a miraculous strength. His eyes then come alive, the wrinkles around them ripple, Printz has wrinkles, he has more and more of them. Printz is getting old.

I'm getting old.

It is the sixth day that Printz has not been out. Herzog and

Matilda occasionally, increasingly often, press their ears to the partition wall. They ask: *When's he going?*

Printz says: *I've run out of milk. I'm leaving today.* He says that in the direction of the partition wall. Printz is clever.

In addition to the torn pages and a few books, Printz puts into his Samsonite briefcase some underwear, his scissors and an Oral-B toothbrush. It is spring.

Printz puts the thirty-two volumes of the *Encyclopædia Britannica* into the large suitcase with wheels, Ernestina's suitcase, red, plastic-coated and rough to the touch. It is an expensive suitcase, robust, transoceanic, with coat-hangers and compartments so that stage dresses do not crush. So that they only crush a little. They are ironed in the hotels in any case. Ernestina is dead. There are no more stage dresses.

Leave that suitcase, says Matilda. *I need that suitcase.* She says that standing in the doorway, with her hands on her hips. Her hair is in rollers because ever since Ernestina died, she has been rolling her hair up, it is full of curls, her head is covered in blond ringlets that touch her cheeks.

Fuck you, says Printz.

Maybe Printz does not say "fuck you" just like that? Maybe Printz would have screwed Matilda, she irritated him so much that he might have screwed her, and that is why he said "fuck you." But Printz is in a hurry, he cannot think about what Freud might have said, he cannot elaborate on that little indecent thought, that little desecrating thought, even perhaps a bit incestuous. Printz is in a hurry, he is in a hurry because Herzog and Matilda are driving him out of his father's flat, out of the flat which his father Rikard Dvorsky was given in exchange for the Villa Nora, that is why he is in a hurry.

Printz goes to the small hunchbacked dealer with knobbly fingers and white hairs in his ears and nose. The small hunchbacked dealer is a talkative dealer, like a magician, he pulls antique ornaments once in the possession of wealthy and murdered Jewish families out of a heap of piled up objects. Maybe Printz really would have screwed blue-eyed Matilda, that cow with a dried-up udder. He had not screwed anything for a long time. Why had Printz not fucked for so long?

I'm getting ready like a cicada. In the little cage of a long-dead sophist, I'm waiting for the sun to warm me.

Printz is sluggish again, sometimes he seizes up.

I'm tired.

There is no inner liveliness in Printz, he is sinking and vanishing like foam. When he makes holes in himself with his scissors and waits for milk to pour out of his little holes, but there is no milk, only blood that scrawls over his torso in quiet, thin little paths, he is not lively even then, no. He is turning into Pupi, that is all.

Fuck you, Matilda, says Printz again and Herzog asks:

What have you taken?

I'm going, says Printz. And asks: *Where are Ernestina's dresses?*

Printz is not sure whether Herzog asks him anything else, because he is already on the stairs, he is going down, he is dragging Ernestina's suitcase, crammed full of books.

The dealer whom Printz had engaged to find out whether there were any living descendants of the Leder family, the original owners of the silver salvers from the confiscated Villa Nora, is called Ugo Tutzman. Ugo Tutzman telephones Printz while he is drinking milk in his pyjamas for a week and says: *Come at once.* It is 1996, perhaps 1997. Printz can no longer say confidently what year it is because time is getting smudged in his head.

I have temporal blotches in my brain.

Printz is aware of those blotches in his brain; they spread like a crumbled cow pie, they are dark as cattle droppings, they spread, flow, cling, cover his brain cells, they are odorless.

Leder, you say, says the dealer Ugo Tutzman. It is stuffy in the room, the blinds are down and rotting.

Did you manage to sell the silverware? asks Printz.

No, says Ugo Tutzman. *I found some distant relatives. I'll tell you everything. In detail.*

Printz does not want to listen. He is not interested in a detailed account of the Jewish family, in whose house, after the war, the victorious communist government installed his father, the chemist, communist and spy Rikard Dvorsky. He is not interested in that. Printz just wants to sell the silverware or give it away because it is in his way. What? Who's Benjamin Vukas?

No need to go into detail, says Printz.

Printz does not want any particulars, either verbal or physical, he does not know what to do with them. He has decided to remove particulars from his life. That is why he is clearing up, clearing out.

Ugo Tutzman is very insistent. He talks while Printz sits on a Louis XVI chair. The chair is rickety and covered in crimson velour, worn. Printz is not comfortable on the Louis XVI chair. He wriggles.

I'm not comfortable on this chair, he says.

Perhaps you would like some tea? asks Ugo Tutzman.

Oh, why does this man mention tea! Pupi cannot bear tea, any kind of tea. He can only bear milk. And wine. White wine, or perhaps red, he can increasingly bear wine but that does not stop him from still drinking milk, no, Pupi adores milk and will never give it up. Unless he really must.

I'd like to sit on your bergère, I like that bergère, says Printz.

Ugo Tutzman is sitting on the bergère. It is covered in stripes of black and white satin, horizontal. It is shabby too, that bergère, soaked with greasy stains and time. Everything at Ugo Tutzman's is dilapidated and shabby. Ugo Tuzman is shabby too. He is also half-blind.

I've got glaucoma, he says.

That's an insidious disease, says Printz. *Hereditary. I would prefer not to listen to your story.*

It's an exciting story, says Ugo Tutzman. *It contains a little enigma. I've brought the Encyclopædia Britannica. It has 32 volumes. It's an expensive complete set. Preserved. A few pages are missing, but no one would know. Palm my set off on someone. I'll call in from time to time, maybe I'll bring some other things. Do you need paintings? Let a bit of light into the room. I'd prefer not to hear your story. I know it all. I know as much as I need.*

I've heard about a person from the Leder family, says Ugo Tutzman.

I could bring you a small Babić, an Aralica from 1935, quite atypical, 100% original, I have Tartalja and Ćelebonović, says Printz.

The man is called Eugen Vukas, and he is the son of Benjamin Vukas.

Who is Benjamin Vukas? asks Printz Dvorsky.

I've just told you. Benjamin Vukas is dead. Eugen Vukas is his son. Eugen Vukas brought me some old photographs. He said, try to sell them, they are very rare, Ugo Tutzman waves the photographs around in the dark room. Raising dust. There is a lot of dust in the room. It is mostly the dust of the past.

Ugo Tutzman does not understand: Printz is not interested in the photographs of Eugen Vukas, Printz is busy:

In addition to the Encyclopædia, in this red case there are several old books of almost antique value. It is my mother's suitcase, you know. It's the suitcase she had for her travels, for her performances. But she is dead, so she doesn't travel anymore, she doesn't perform. She used to sing. Perhaps you have some milk? I'd prefer to drink a glass of milk. I don't like tea. These are small prewar books: The Palace of the Poor; Clown; The Crisis of Bourgeois Democracy; Stalin: On Lenin.

Ugo Tutzman: *Benjamin Vukas was a friend of the Leder family. That letter "H" in the monogram "HL" on your trays and cutlery, represents the name "Hedda."*

Printz: *Hedda means "war." In Greek.*

Ugo Tutzman: *Benjamin Vukas had a daughter, Julijana, and that son, Eugen. Benjamin Vukas worked in a Mr. Cohen's photography studio. The studio was called Jacques. The daughter died as a Partisan fighter in 1944, somewhere in Bosnia, in 1942, the studio was confiscated, but Eugen is still alive, and old.*

Printz: *Don't heat it. I like cold milk.*

Ugo Tutzman: *Julijana Vukas had a friend, Isabella Fischer, whose mother was called Sonja and her maiden name was Leder. Otherwise, the Leder family lived in Chemnitz.*

Printz: *In socialist days, Chemnitz was called Karl-Marx-Stadt. Now it's Chemnitz again.*

Ugo Tutzman: *Sonja Leder, married name Fischer, had a sister, Hedda. Their paternal grandfather, owner of a leather processing factory, built the Villa Nora in 1880. The factory was also called Leder.*

Printz: *In a glass if possible. It's best to drink cold milk from a glass. It's logical that the factory should be called Leder, that's logical, isn't it?*

Ugo Tutzman: *In 1940, Sonja Leder, married name Fischer, came to visit her sister Hedda, with her daughter Isabella. Naturally they stayed in the Villa Nora. Isabella left with Julijana Vukas, Julijana Vukas died.*

Printz: *So you said.*

Ugo Tutzman: *But Isabella crossed onto the island of Korčula, then to Bari. Her mother, Sonja Fischer, née Leder, went back to her husband in Chemnitz. In Bari Isabella met her future husband, Felix Rosenzweig, co-owner of a chocolate factory in Austria.*

Printz: *Lucky. Felix means Lucky.*

Ugo Tutzman: *Isabella and Felix live in Salzburg.*

Printz: *Mozart kugeln are made in Salzburg.*

Ugo Tutzman: *Isabella's husband dies at the end of the nineteen-seventies and she moves back over here.*

Printz: *Where over here?*

Ugo Tutzman: *Isabella finds Benjamin Vukas and in his name opens a photographic salon Bon-bon.*

Printz: *I don't like bonbons. Especially not chocolates. They make me constipated. Except maybe the ones filled with cherries and cognac. They are good. Bonbons with marzipan are also good.*

Ugo Tutzman: *Eugen Vukas claims that Isabella Fischer, married name Rosenzweig, is the only one of her family to have survived the Holocaust. There are no more Leders or Fischers. In other words, this silverware could belong to her. Eugen Vukas is prepared to find Isabella Fischer although since his father Benjamin Vukas died, he has no news of Isabella Fischer.*

Printz does not want to listen to Ugo Tutzman. He has more important business and Ugo Tutzman exhausts him. Printz sips the cold milk that Ugo Tutzman brings him, but the glass is small and greasy and that revolts Printz. That is why he drinks slowly. Who is Benjamin Vukas? Who is Eugen Vukas? What have they to do with his life? What is this Ugo Tutzman talking about? Printz no longer wants to listen to Jewish stories, when he hears Jewish stories, little animals come into his head. Then come out of his head. And gaze at him. Or crawl over him.

One louse creeps over the back of his neck. Printz puts his thumb and forefinger under his open collar, catches it, that louse, turns its body, soft, but still brittle as a grain of rice, turns it between his thumb and forefinger and then lets it drop. Does it want to live or die, wonders Printz. Cornelius a Lapide says that lice were created from human sweat, and not made by god on the sixth day with the other animals. The itching on his neck annoys Printz, irritates him. the life of his body, badly dressed, badly fed, a body eaten by lice, drives him to close his eyes and he, Printz, shuts his eyes in a sudden spasm of despair and in the darkness he sees the shiny brittle bodies of lice falling out of the air and twisting rapidly in their fall.

Printz wants to leave Ugo Tutzman's warehouse. He wants to go. In Ugo Tutzman's warehouse Printz loses his identity. He knows that he is called Printz Dvorsky and not Stephen Dedalus, he knows that, but still, he feels, he sees lice crawling over his body, emerging not just from his collar but out of his sleeves, the seams of his trousers, and Printz is afraid that they might reach his eyes, as happens when he is attacked by ants. Or worms.

I'm going, says Printz. *I lose my identity here.*

Eugen Vukas is very old, he's eighty, says Ugo Tutzman. *Before the war he helped his father Benjamin in Mr. Cohen's photography studio. The studio was called Jacques. After the war, he had several different jobs but never worked as a photographer again. He worked in a public kitchen, in a leather company, in a sugar factory, he was a dealer in eggs and manager of a traveling circus.*

This biography, this little biography, seems familiar to Printz. He does not want to listen anymore, absolutely not. That is why Prinz tells Ugo Tutzman: *You've got your lives mixed up. That's someone else's life.*

Maybe, says Ugo Tutzman and his eyes water. From glaucoma and dust and the dark and old age. They are soft tears, amorphous, like puddles, they are not pretty, clear and round. Ugo Tutzman's tears are not the limpid tears produced by young eyes, they are the opaque tears of the old.

You have ugly tears, says Printz.

Ugo Tutzman says: *They aren't tears, they're a reflex.* Then he adds: *Maybe none of us has his own life. Is your life unconditionally yours?*

Sell my books and send the silver to that Isabella, says Printz and leaves Ugo Tutzman's dark room. It is dark outside as well, but it is still spring. Outside there is springtime darkness. Some would say—a mild spring night.

I'll come by to pick up my pension, says Printz to his brother Herzog.

It'll be waiting for you in the mailbox, says Herzog to his brother Printz. *Your pension will be waiting for you in the mailbox,* Herzog says again so that there is no misunderstanding.

So he goes. Printz. He goes.

It is a lair, we know. There are lairs like this all over the world, they resemble each other. There are also quite a few lair-people, they are all over the place, it is nothing new, they resemble each other and their lives in their lairs are on the whole similar although

I'm a little white weasel in a traveling cage. The cage has a handle and is easy to carry. It has bars I look out through. Through which I sniff the outside world. It could not be said that I am imprisoned. No. I'm not imprisoned. The little white weasel came of its own accord. I close the door from inside and I can go out whenever I wish. Sometimes I do. I dream in the cage. In the cage I sometimes grow, sometimes I shrink. When I grow, I grow big as a horse. I become a big horse, a transparent horse, I become a glass horse, fragile, invisible. But big. When I shrink, I become a cicada.

The lair is that hiding-place in the park behind the fortress, near the zoo. During the day, Printz walks, at night he reads. He reads his notes, the torn-out pages from books, all that he managed to bring with him. He reads by candlelight, Printz bought a heap of candles for reading. When it gets cold,

it's not cold yet, it's still spring, then summer will come, then autumn, winter's a way off

when it gets cold, Printz goes to reading rooms. To the city reading rooms, local and foreign, there are foreign reading rooms in the city, it is a big city. There is a French, a British and a German reading room. The German reading room is named after Goethe. In the city there are several reading rooms of various kinds. It is warm in doctors' surgeries as well. In the surgeries Printz waits in line. As he waits, he reads. Sometimes he sleeps. Printz takes care of his health. He has his blood pressure measured. He monitors his blood count. Monitors his eyesight. Sight is important to Printz, very important, because of reading. Sometimes Printz buys vitamins. He buys foreign vitamins, he does not want to buy locally produced vitamins. He does not know why.

Don't throw away your old newspapers, Printz says to the women in the reading rooms. In all the reading rooms, the employees are women. In both the foreign and local reading rooms, nothing but women. *Give me your old newspapers.*

Printz uses the old newspapers to line his lair, his shoes and in winter, his body. Printz is also given magazines with headlines in color. Magazines are too short for lining the lair but the color headlines are nice because they do not leak ink. They are foreign magazines.

Over and over again.

For five years.

For five years.

For five years.

Five years.

Five.

Printz knows what is happening in the world. He keeps up. He keeps up with wars and he keeps up with culture. And the discovery of the human genome. And extra-uterine conception. Sperm donors. He keeps up with insanity. With everything. That is why he is not like anyone else, he is special. Pupi.

He visits the animals. He does not converse with them. No.

I'd like to have a laptop. Battery-driven.

When it is warm and dry outside, Printz goes barefoot. He still has those Florsheim shoes, the black ones, brogues. Florsheim shoes are indestructible.

I've got some Bally loafers as well, I'm saving them.

Printz has a pair of Bally shoes hidden under a heap of newspapers in his residential hole in the park.

When I get back on my feet, I'll buy some Paciotti boots. Two pairs.

Printz goes to exhibitions. Printz knows that he will not see Maristella at those exhibitions. Maristella is at other exhibitions, far away,

but not that far away

nevertheless, Printz goes to exhibitions, almost regularly, in autumn and spring. Not in winter. Exhibitions open when it gets dark and from the street, they look cinematic because they have large display windows, brightly lit. Inside, the exhibitions contain some people Printz knows. Printz endeavors to go to the exhibitions spruced up but his Burberry has seen better days. His Burberry is full of wine and *burek* pie stains, Printz adores *burek* pies, especially meat ones because of the onion taste. Afterward, he belches.

I sometimes have stomach problems.

His beige Burberry is crumpled, in fact it is already an old raincoat, the hem has come undone and hangs down. Its collar is greasy, really greasy, black. Printz is paid a small pension, small. It sometimes happens, when he calls around for it, for his pension, that it is not in the mailbox. It sometimes happens that he just finds a little note, saying: *We borrowed your pension, we'll return it next month. Herzog.* It sometimes happens that they do not return it. Then difficult days, months, ensue. Nonetheless, when he goes to exhibitions, Printz cuts his nails. When he does not go to exhibitions, he does not cut his nails, they are long and dirty. But Printz has his hair cut regularly. Mostly regularly. His hair has thinned. He is not bald, his hair has just thinned. Printz will not go bald, he is one of those people who do not go bald. Printz has two Pierre Cardin shirts, white. They are worn out too, especially the collars and cuffs, but on the whole they are clean, even pressed, on the whole. He has retained that from his past, cleanliness in clothes and body although he has increasingly frequent lapses. When sadness comes over him, then he lapses, then Printz looks terrible.

What kind of sadness?

Planetary. Familial. Personal.

That's claptrap. I've changed my theory of life, I've recognized my priorities.

He has changed his theory of life, he has recognized his priorities.

Printz takes his shirts to a laundry, with his underpants, which are also washed out and torn, with holes in them. When he does not go to exhibitions, Printz does not wear white shirts, no way. He has a cotton T-shirt, gray-black, anthracite. Printz likes the gray-black color and he is fond of his dirty T-shirt, he is fond of it.

Yes.

Besides, before he falls asleep in his lair, Printz twists the ends of that T-shirt. That is a hangover from his past as well, from his childhood. He twists a bit of hair, a bit of the edge of his T-shirt and falls asleep. On the newspapers.

So, at exhibitions, Printz does not look like a vagrant, no. Only he does not wear socks. Printz does not wear socks and that looks odd, especially in winter, but in the winter he does not go to exhibitions so there is no one to wonder about it. It is only at exhibitions that Printz might come across a familiar face. He avoids the other places where he might come across a familiar face. Nonetheless, not wearing socks gives Printz away. Not wearing socks suggests that perhaps something should be done. Wearing shoes on bare feet might be fashionable in summer, but not in winter. At public gatherings, some people give Printz a wide berth. Some do not. Some observe him although they pretend they have not seen him, they watch him surreptitiously, head down. Because, there is a difference, there is. Printz today and before, those are irreconcilable images, irreconcilable. And the city is not exactly so big that people do not know each other. Some people.

Don't talk crap.

At exhibitions they serve canapés with red or black caviar, there is champagne. Printz likes that. Printz has refined taste, educated taste. It just happened that way. At exhibitions there is Roquefort and Camembert. There are slices of smoked salmon coiled into little flowers, into little fishy roses. There is roast beef, dark pink inside, as it should be, sometimes there are slices of Wellington, prawns with sauce or without, sometimes mignon,

I don't eat mignon

there is excellent wine, from the islands, what are you doing, Pupi?

Psshht.

Printz takes two unopened bottles of wine and tucks them into the inner pocket of his Burberry. That is intolerable! Printz takes a bottle of red and a bottle of white.

so they won't be missed.

The bottles clink like small bells, softly. They clink in Pupi's inside pocket. Printz:

So what! Althusser used to steal. He stole small things around the shops of Brittany.

Althusser. It would be better for Printz not to mention Althusser. Althusser killed his wife Hélène Rytmann, he suffocated her while massaging the vertebrae in her neck. Then he spent three years in hospital.

Althusser did not kill Rytmann. He helped her to kill herself because she wanted to kill herself. After that Althusser lost some of his reputation and influence. But his former students, Balibar and Rancière, did not reject him, no. Philosophers are lonely creatures Althusser used to say, he could never understand what people saw in Foucault's defini-

*tion of insanity. Foucault was Althusser's former student too. Foucault
was therefore younger than Althusser, but he died before him, Althusser.
They were both bipolar. Foucault died in 1984, bald. Althusser was
born in 1918. Rikard was born in 1918. Rikard is my father. Althusser
died before my father. My father is called Rikard. He is dead. Althusser
died in 1990, and Rikard five or six years later. Foucault was born
in 1926. He was fifty-eight when he closed his eyes. He closed his eyes
forever in hospital. That sounds good: closing one's eyes forever. Foucault died of AIDS and shaved his head like Yul Brynner who died of
cancer. After Brynner's death, the Yul Brynner Foundation was set up
for the treatment of carcinoma of the head and neck. Althusser does not
have a foundation named after him. Nor does Foucault. They did not
die of cancer. Yul Brynner was born on the island of Sakhalin, in Russia. Yul Brynner had Romani blood, he played the balalaika in a Paris
nightclub and was a trapeze artist. Yul Brynner studied for a while
at the Sorbonne. It is possible that Althusser and Brynner passed one
another in the streets of Paris and it is possible that they did not. When
Foucault appeared, Brynner was already in America, so the two bald
men could not have met. Yul Brynner was better looking than Foucault. Now they are both dead. Foucault died of AIDS and Brynner of
cancer. Sorry? I've already said that? Foucault had various lovers, and
Umberto Eco wrote a novel Foucault's Pendulum which has nothing
to do with Michel Foucault but is about the physicist Jean-Bernard-
Léon Foucault from the 19th century. Michel Foucault belonged to the
20th century. Umberto Eco recently published a new novel Baudalino.
The action takes place in Alessandria, Eco was born in Alessandria
and Baudalino was the protector of that little town, which is incidentally where Borsalino hats come from. Alessandria was famous for its
good-looking girls. Alessandria is in Lombardy. Serbian officers from
the Austro-Hungarian army serving in barracks in Lombardy used to
go to Alessandria. They went to look for women as the little town was
known for its good-looking girls. I'm not married.*

Printz is standing in the middle of a gallery talking. It is impossible to stop him. Printz has not spoken for a long time, not to anyone, to no one, for a very long time, and now he is exploiting the opportunity. If they wish, these people can listen to him, if they do not, they can go. He will talk, he will talk as long as his thoughts keep coming, Printz has a lot of thoughts, those are perfectly okay coherent thoughts, they are often intelligent thoughts, Printz knows that.

I haven't slept for a long time. A week. That's why I'm talking.

Some guests are smiling with evident discomfort on their faces, they shift from foot to foot, some pick leftovers from the table, others pay no attention to Printz, they converse as though he was not there. Printz still has no intention of stopping. Whenever the clamor increases, he raises his voice. In a corner someone with a mobile phone calls an ambulance. What shall we do with him?

With whom?

As soon as structuralism became fashionable, Althusser took it up with enthusiasm. In addition, Althusser was a member of the French Communist Party. Later he persuaded Foucault to sign up. Althusser joined the Party in 1948 and Foucault in 1950. Both of them later signed out. 1948 was an awkward year, the year of the Informbiro. My father Rikard did not mess up. In hospital they stuffed Althusser with drugs that were not innocuous. They told him, "Mr. Althusser, you are a manic-depressive, you are bipolar." Althusser said: "What can be done, I was born in Algeria." Althusser was born in Algeria. He was a Marxist who criticized Marx. He rejected the Marxist theory of economic determinism; he rejected the idea that economic systems determined the organization of society, its political and intellectual reality. For Althusser, Marxism was not a moral philosophy concerned with man's alienation in capitalism and his salvation in socialism, no. Althusser saw Marxism as an antihumanist science. Althusser wrote a lot about the relationship between art and ideology; about the relation-

ship between the individual and institutions. According to Althusser, man is an ideological being, man is shit, therefore ideology, or ideological state apparatuses, influence all aspects of society, including art.

These paintings of yours are naked ideology, pernicious and hollow. This art of yours is no good! says Printz, in fact he is already shouting.

The ambulance does not come. Printz carries on. Now he is going to toss Foucault in, obviously.

Do you know what ideology is? It's an activity that permeates the whole of society; all groups and all classes participate in it voluntarily. That's why it's impossible to overthrow tyrants and dictators, that's why. That's why tyrants endure, for at least ten years, but they always carry on longer than that, far longer. If they don't die of cancer. Or heart problems. Or old age. What do you mean repression? Repression is your choice, your food. Your pictures. You are inside. If you want to get out, prisons, madhouses, and hospitals await you. Now we've come to Foucault, the unfortunate Foucault who could not stand his father, the surgeon. My father was a chemist. There's no genuine knowledge. Knowledge is determined by power, power manages knowledge. The humanist, ostensibly reforming institutions of the nineteenth century, were despotic institutions. They subordinated their spirit to the surveillance of cultural norms. Various technologies control our mind and body. That's what Foucault maintains, not me. I agree. Althusser persuaded Foucault to join the communist party. He fucked up. The communists said that homosexuality was a vice and consequence of bourgeois decadence. One of Foucault's lovers was the composer Jean Barraqué. Foucault adored the word archaeology. *Everything was archaeology to him. He was forever digging.*

Has someone called an ambulance? When it comes, they will take me to a madhouse, and a madhouse—this is what Foucault says—is a place where people are accused, where they are judged, a place out of which there is no escape without repentance. I shall not repent. In a madhouse, madness is punished even when that madness is completely innocuous outside the madhouse. Like mine. My father was a chemist. He was called Rikard. He agreed to give his chemistry a political status and his chemistry became the faithful servant of ideology. Power models our souls. Look at yourselves! I was punished by my father. I had to kneel. Kneeling is like penitence. I knelt for hours with my face turned toward the corner of a room, not to the wall, but a corner. On maize kernels. I had to apologize. I had to say forgive me, I did wrong, forgive me. He sent me to bed without supper. When I did not agree with my father, even if that disagreement was about some chemical question, insignificant, because chemical questions are on the whole insignificant, I am a chemist too, but I didn't want to be a chemist, so when I didn't agree with Rikard, he would say: "I'll pierce your tongue with needles. I'll pierce your tongue with needles." With needles. How many needles did he have in mind? How much of the surface of my tongue did he intend to pierce with needles, how much? Did he intend to leave those needles in my tongue, leave them sticking out of it until he decided to remove them? How deeply did he intend to push those needles into my tongue? There is a lot a blood in a tongue. The tongue bleeds when it is injured, but it does not bleed for long, that's one good thing, that's the good thing about a bloody tongue. Saliva stops the blood, saliva is antiseptic, it coats the tongue so it doesn't bleed for long. The tongue stretches deep into the throat. My father didn't pierce my tongue with needles, but he said he was going to. There, that's Foucault. Where's that ambulance? I'm tired.

At the hospital, Printz tells the doctor: *Everything's under control. Give me a bed. I'll be good, I'll be quiet.*

Printz sleeps for 72 hours without stirring. He sleeps for as long as he had stayed awake without a break. Now he was back in form.

I'm as good as new.

Don't worry, says the doctor. *Now you're good as new. Do a bit more walking.*

But, Printz is worried. He's worried because he can feel an attack of satyriasis coming on, he has occasional attacks of satyriasis. When the attacks pass, Printz is calm for a long time, there is nothing, no urges. Indeed, Printz is then largely dead, as far as urges go.

Sexually speaking, insects have the most staying power. They stay conjoined for several hours and as soon as they separate, they die. Cicadas are insects. There is a type of insect as small as a grain of rice, they're known as lovebugs (*Plecia nearctica*), because most of them are in Florida. They only live for 150 hours and spend 56 of those hours conjoined, without a pause.

Printz's attacks of satyriasis are paltry compared to the urge and potency of some animals. So, it is stupid for Printz to get upset, to be worried, he knows that. It is stupid that the doctor says *take up sport and go to concerts,* he always says that, he'll say it today as well. When chimpanzees have an attack of satyriasis, they fuck 60 times a day. Lions screw up to 30 times a day, sables 30 times in 18 hours, rats shag up to 500 times in 6 hours, pheasants—100 times in 12 hours, and bulls hump 30 times a day.

Of course, all these animals do not fornicate constantly. They bonk intensively satyriatically, only when they are imprisoned, when they live in zoos, when they are bored and when it is the season for mating, only then.

I feel like fucking something, says Printz.

Go to a concert. If possible a piano or violin recital. Piano and violin recitals are soothing. Avoid orchestral concerts. That's what the doctor tells Printz.

Violins irritate me, says Printz. *They remind me of my life.*

There are a lot of lives like yours, it isn't anything terrible. The doctor does not give up. The doctor is a completely modern type. *Cole Porter, for instance …*

Cole Porter fell off a horse, he had his right leg amputated, after a manic spell, he fell into a depression and he was rich, says Printz.

He was a rich homo. Do you play any instrument? the doctor asks

Printz. *That would be good. People should play instruments.*

There are a lot of street buskers these days. There are a lot of mu-sicians with similar lives. And there are some with different lives.
I'm not a homo, says Printz. *A delicate madness accompanies many musicians.*

The doctor agrees: *Ronnie Scott—a man of delicate madness.*

and many writers, says Printz.

and many painters, says the doctor.

One should believe Printz, he studies other people's lives. And one should believe the doctor, he studies other people's lives too. Printz and the doctor believe each other. They know each other. They meet from time to time, especially in winter, when Printz is cold in the hole near the zoo, when he feels cold and dirty so he drinks stolen wine, and wanders around as he did last night. Then the doctor takes him in.

Take Bruckner, says the doctor. *Bruckner adored young ladies.*

Graham Greene slept with forty-seven prostitutes, says Printz. Then he adds: *I won't go to a concert, I don't like concerts.*

Doctor: *Graham Greene was a friend of Kim Philby.*

Printz: *I have things in common with Graham Greene. Graham Greene is dead. Graham Greene met Castro and Ho Chi Minh. I met Tito and Suharto.*

Doctor: *Many people have things in common. Hugo Wolf had things in common ... Hugo Wolf*

Printz: *Born in Slovenj Gradec in 1860, died in Vienna 1903.*

Doctor: *Infected with syphilis as a young man.*

Printz: *Hector Berlioz had thick red hair*

Doctor: *and ended up as a librarian.*

Printz: *Mussorgsky*

Doctor: *Scriabin*

Printz: *Rachmaninoff*

Doctor: *Tchaikovsky*

Printz: *epileptic*
Doctor: *Handel*
Printz: *Schumann*
Doctor: *Rossini*
Printz: *Jaco Pastorius*
Doctor: *Vagrant. Drug addict. Suicide.*
Printz: *Kurt Cobain. Suicide.*
Doctor: *Literature!*
Printz: *Kleist. Suicide.*
Doctor: *Hans Christian Andersen.*
Printz: *Malcolm Lowry, hospitalization, suicide.*
Doctor: *Ibsen.*
Printz: *Chatterton—suicide, Celan—suicide*
Doctor: *Balzac.*
Printz: *Faulkner, hospitalization.*
Doctor: *Fitzgerald, hospitalization.*
Printz: *Hesse.*
Doctor: *Tennessee Williams, hospitalization.*
Printz: *William Inge, suicide, Splendor in the Grass, Natalie Wood and Warren Beatty, rivers of alcohol, Come Back, Little Sheba, more alcohol. Little Sheba is a dog.*
Doctor: *Maxim Gorky, attempted suicide.*
Printz: *Hemingway, suicide, Virginia Woolf listens to sparrows singing in Ancient Greek, hospitalization, suicide.*
Doctor: *Gogol.*
Printz: *Conrad, attempted suicide.*
Doctor: *Mark Twain, Charles Dickens, Tolstoy, Melville, Turgenev.*
Printz: *John Berryman, suicide.*
Doctor: *?*
Printz: *I am the little man who smokes and smokes.*
I am the girl who does know better but.
I am the king of the pool.

I am so wise I had my mouth sewn shut.

Doctor: *?*

Printz: *Phenomenal memory. Father—suicide under his window. Alcoholism. Jumps from a bridge.*

Doctor: *Strindberg, Zola, Henry James.*

Printz: *Eugene O'Neill, hospitalization, attempted suicide.*

Doctor: *Artaud, hospitalization.*

Printz: *Baudelaire, attempted suicide.*

Doctor: *Byron, T. S. Eliot, Alexander Blok.*

Printz: *Yesenin, Hart Crane, suicide, suicide, Gérard de Nerval, suicide, Mayakovsky, suicide.*

Doctor: *Blake.*

Printz: *Sylvia Plath, suicide, Cesare Pavese, suicide*

Doctor: *Torquato Tasso, Pasternak, Shelley.*

Printz: *Poe, attempted suicide, Roethke, suicide, Tsvetaeva, suicide. Borowski, suicide.*

Doctor: *Churchill!*

Printz: *Lincoln. Idi Amin.*

Doctor: *Vivien Leigh!*

Printz: *Spencer Tracy. Robin Williams.*

Doctor: *Dick Cavett.*

Printz: *Painters.*

Doctor: *I don't have much idea about painters.*

Printz: *Van Gogh, suicide, Testa, suicide by drowning, de Stäel, suicide.*

Doctor: *Michelangelo?*

Printz: *Yes.*

Doctor: *Gauguin?*

Printz: *Yes. Rothko, suicide.*

Doctor: *Munch? Modigliani?*

Printz: *That's enough.*

Doctor: *What about sculptors?*

Printz: *There are hardly any bipolar sculptors. I've had enough.*

Doctor: *There, all great people with things in common, delicate madness, manic-depressive. Humanity is in their debt.*

A nurse comes into the clinic. Printz knows, he is going to have an injection, he will have medication, his satyriasis will disappear, his loquacity will dry up, his sleepiness will grow and then for a long time he will not think. Printz does not complain. He has been washed. He has been fed. He has had enough sleep.

I've had enough sleep.

The nurse says nothing.

Maybe I'll go to a concert after all. It's warm at concerts.

The nurse says nothing.

I saw yellow roses in a shop window, says Printz. *They were artificial roses made of silk, with plastic dew drops. They looked wonderful.*

Printz knows the zoo keepers. He drinks stolen wine and bought beer with them, he shares cheap, only cheap drinks with them. Then they spend time together, Printz and the keepers. The keepers are Printz's friends, Printz's new friends. Printz likes them.

They are my friends.

Printz does not drink brandy, Printz has never drunk brandy, especially not made from plums, Printz does not like plums. He would sometimes drink grappa in Italy, so as not to insult his Italian partners, Italian chemist-spies.

Italian chemists wear Paciotti shoes, Moreschi or Gravati shoes. Some wear Aldo Brue shoes. All Italian chemists' shoes shine, Italian shoes in general are very shiny.

Cognac, yes, Printz likes cognac in small quantities, after dinner. Sometimes Printz feels like French cognac, oh yes, out of a fine wide glass, in a club, in an elegant club, it could be a French club, or an English club, it could be a chemists' club, a spies' club, it could be a club where artists get together, painters, he fits into all kinds of groups, he feels like company, he feels like getting together, he Printz, where is Maristella?

I fit in well. I haven't fitted in for ages. I'd like to fit in again. Is it too late?

Printz's pension is incomprehensibly small because Printz is in fact a bit young for a pension, that is why his pension is small, and also the pension funds are empty, plundered.

I've got a pauper's pension, presumably it's my fault.

It is impossible to live on that pension. It is a Balkan pension. *Transitional.*

Printz mainly uses the pension to buy drink, what can he do. If a bit of money is left, he gives it to beggars. Printz likes giving.

I like to give. Oh, Maristella, I would give you yellow artificial roses with drops of plastic dew.

The zoo keepers sometimes give Printz their old clothes, blue, overalls. The keepers sometimes hide Printz in the storeroom and let him sleep there, secretly.

You can sleep here, they tell him.

The storeroom stinks of animals. Printz puts the piled up working clothing under his head, the floor is wooden.

Printz is going to go back to Ugo Tutzman. It is five years since he last visited Ugo Tutzman. He has to go there to take back at least one volume of his *Encyclopædia Britannica* so that he has something to leaf through in the big storeroom at the zoo, in the winter. Printz has not read anything for a long time. He will go to Ugo Tutzman, yes.

Printz is no longer allowed into the reading rooms.

It's nice there. They won't let me in.

We do not let tramps in, they tell him. *Or the homeless,* say the women between clenched teeth.

Your mouth's like an asshole, says Printz and leaves. Printz always leaves. Printz does not quarrel, he is not a quarrelsome type, he is gentle. In reading rooms and libraries there are always women at the desk.

The *Britannica* would be handy for Printz under his head because his neck gets stiff,

his neck vertebrae are fucked

his worker overalls stink like a billy goat

priests stink like billy goats, village priests particularly

perhaps it is me?

So, Printz lies in the storeroom, thinking. In the morning he asks the keepers: *Where are the rhinos?*

The keepers say: *Sleeping.*

Printz says: *They sleep a lot.*

The keepers say: *They were self-destructive. We put them to sleep.*

Printz says: *Will they wake up?*

The keepers say: *When they wake up, they will be tame.*

Then Printz says: *I'm going. People pass by my cage and don't notice me.*

It is winter. February 2001. Printz is completely rootless. Printz loves white sweaters.

White sweaters really suit me. In white sweaters I am very handsome. I could get some socks.

There is snow, Printz's feet are frozen, he is frozen all over, Printz has no sweater, the Burberry is not warm. The wind blows. Printz has no socks at all. His Florsheim shoes have holes in the soles. Printz is dirty. It is the sixth year of Printz's wandering. The sixth.

I'd like to have nice boots. Black. Leather. Not Florsheim, I'm sick of Florsheim footwear. They could be Bally boots or Salamander boots or solid Austrian boots from the Ludwig Reiter workshop, lined with fur, with thick rubber soles, oh, I'd be able to walk and walk, I could survive: the Austrians make robust goods.

Printz seems to be waking up.

He says: *I'm going to Ugo Tutzman. I haven't been there for a long time.*

At Ugo Tutzman's Ugo Tutzman tells Printz: *I haven't seen you in a long time and I have news.*

Do you have any warm boots? asks Printz.

I've found Isabella Fischer, married name Rosenzweig. I sent her your silverware, the trays and cutlery through a foreigner. I have contacts with foreigners, do you know that? says Ugo Tutzman.

Are you Catholic? asks Printz.

That foreigner brought it all back. Isabella Fischer died. She no longer exists. Here are your goods, says Ugo Tutzman.

I'd like a spoon, silver, and some money, says Printz. *You haven't got any boots?*

You can have lunch with me, you can do that, suggests Ugo Tutzman.

I'd like that, says Printz. *I'd like to eat with this silver cutlery. I live in a hole, you know, in a cage.*

Ugo Tutzman and Printz eat in silence. They eat thick vegetable soup and a lot of bread. The bread is warm because Ugo Tutzman keeps it wrapped in aluminum foil on his tiled stove. It is warm in the room as well.

We had a tiled stove when I went to kindergarten, says Printz. *Your stove takes me back to my childhood.*

After they have eaten, Ugo Tutzman says: *I'll give you a bottle of original French cognac in exchange for your silverware.*

Printz says: *That would make me happy. I'm a connoisseur of cognac. Cognac is living matter. Cognac is the taste of happiness. Cognac transforms all ordinariness into exaltation, and exaltation is the sublimation of beauty. Cognac is sublimation. Lobster and crêpes Suzette flambées in cognac. Do you know Maristella?*

Cognac ferments. The best cognac takes decades to come into its own. Cognac needs time and moisture and special oak barrels. There is no bouquet without oak. Now I understand, I actually adore cognac. Cognac is the servant of time. The last phase in the maturation of cognac is oxidation. Oxidation comes after hydrolysis. Give me the right con-

ditions, I'll make cognac for you. Do you know Maristella?

I prefer liqueurs, says Ugo Tutzman. *I adore Benedictine.*

Deo Optimo Maximo, said the Benedictine Don Bernardo Vincelli and made his elixir from 27 kinds of herb, says Printz. *That was the beginning of the sixteenth century in the Fécamp monastery. Nowadays Fécamp is a tourist destination. I could tell you various religious stories.*

I'm not a believer, Mr. Dvorsky, I only sell other people's belongings.

Printz likes Ugo Tutzman. He likes the fact that he is not a believer although he does not like his dark room. Ugo Tutzman's dark room sows disquiet in Printz's soul.

That is why Printz says: *Mr. Tutzman, you are a dear man. Pull up the blinds.*

You are a connoisseur of alcohol, Mr. Dvorsky? asks Ugo Tutzman.

Oh yes, says Printz. Then he adds: *today I feel like Benedict.*

Benedict lived like a hermit in an inaccessible cave above Subiaco, says Ugo Tutzman. *He was visited by a raven and he kept imagining he saw a woman. Then he threw himself into nettles and thorns, completely naked, and rolled around in those thorns, rolled and rolled until he was covered in blood.*

Yes, says Printz. *I keep imagining I see a woman too. And I am covered in blood, but I don't roll around. In recent times I have become less bloody. The recipe for Benedictine was lost during the French Revolution and has no connection with St. Benedict. The recipe was discovered by chance. The liqueur contains saffron, coriander, thyme, juniper, orange peel, infusions, honey. It's a good liqueur. Could you give me that French cognac now, Mr. Tutzman. I should be going.*

Mr. Dvorsky, says Ugo Tutzman, *don't worry, I am alone too.*

The Tarantula cocktail is made from Benedictine. A tarantula is otherwise a deadly spider. It was once thought that the tarantula provokes tarantism, but tarantism is a disease of enforced dancing. A person with that disease twitches. Tarantism is also called chorea, from the Greek—dance and is also called St. Vitus Dance. Do you think that St. Vitus danced?

St. Vitus is the patron saint of some towns, says Ugo Tutzman.

The Tarantula cocktail contains whiskey, vermouth, Benedictine, a little lemon and a lot of ice. The Tarantula cocktail refreshes and warms at the same time. I drank it in Greece. Dogs can get chorea as well. I had a dog that caught chorea. He was called Bufi. He twitched like a puppet on a string. He had to be put down. He was my dog. After that I got a new dog but he was taken away from me too. He was also called Bufi. All my pets were called Bufi, unless they were birds. The birds were called Ćićo. I'm not remotely alone. I'm going, says Printz. *Incidentally, Mr. Tutzman, I have a photographic memory.*

In the monasteries the friars didn't only eat and drink, they adored bloodletting. They had their blood let more than fifteen times a year. After every bloodletting they could eat and drink even more. They became lively. What are you saying, Mr. Dvorsky?

Perhaps Mr. Tutzman knows something? Printz says:

Women take alcohol better than men because the female body contains more moisture. Women have unusually moist bodies.

Who is Maristella? asks Ugo Tutzman.

I feel like a bull, says Printz. *Do you hear the bells? Church bells make me lively. When I hear church bells I feel lively. One could say—angry. I would not wish to be angry now. Is it a feast day?*

The clanging of the church bells produces little images in Printz's brain, swaying images, drunken and red. Those images, clearly framed, come before Printz's eyes, where they multiply and disturb him. That is why Printz feels like a bull and he does not know whether he can explain this to Ugo Tutzman. They are not easily explained phenomena, those images. Here, for instance, swans appear. Swans sail through Printz's brain and as they sail they change color, they are not white swans as in real life, they are special swans from some other world, from a world

Printz does not belong to, from some buried world. Those swans, those red swans, are elusive. With their necks wound into a wreath, in fact into a knot, they sail together, as though imprisoned, Printz is afraid. What if the swans sail out of his head and into Ugo Tutzman's room? What if, with their twisted, bound necks, they start padding around Ugo Tutzman's room? What if they spread their wings? Red swans with their wings stretched could look terrifying. Swans have beaks. What if they start using their sharp beaks to dig at his eyes, to peck at his skull looking for a way out? Ugo Tutzman could take fright and tell Printz *it's time you were going*. Perhaps it really is time for Printz to be going? But Printz enjoys being at Ugo Tutzman's. Ugo Tutzman has given him cognac, if he stays for another hour or two, Ugo Tutzman might be able to find, among his old things, some suitable footwear for him, Printz, his Florsheim shoes have become unusable, there are at least five layers of newspaper in them, they are full of plastic bags, they are too tight for Printz's feet and he could get fungus from the damp.

Fungi might start growing between my toes, says Printz.

Fungal diseases are very tedious, says Ugo Tutzman. *Fungus is hard to cure. Hard to eliminate.*

If there are no shoes for him, perhaps Ugo Tutzman could offer him somewhere to sleep, he could do. It is dark. It is winter. The nights are cold and windy. Printz does not want to go back to that hole anymore. He doesn't want to.

I'd like to stay a bit longer, says Printz. *Who knows when I'll come again.*

I'm not Catholic, says Ugo Tutzman. *I am not a believer. The church bells no longer have any effect on me. None. You can stay the night.*

Oh, how proud of himself Printz is. He had a thought, he had a little wish and he succeeded in realizing his wish. That had not happened to him for a long time, that he had a wish and secured its realization. He had carried out this business about staying the night well, elegantly, he had done it unobtrusively. Ugo Tutzman is a good man. Printz was not mistaken.

I was not mistaken. You are a good man, says Printz.

I'm Estonian, says Ugo Tutzman.

Estonia is known for its black pudding. Would you like us to talk about Estonia? asks Printz.

Estonia separated itself from the Soviet Union in 1991. It is now independent. Estonia is a small country, good for holidays. I have not been to Estonia for a long time. About fifty years, says Ugo Tutzman.

Printz: *The soil is marshy.*

Ugo: *The country is good for long walks.*

Printz: *There are no more coupons for gas or vouchers for food. That has been abolished.*

Ugo: *Estonia is now waiting for tourists, because Estonia is a country the size of Switzerland and there are no more lines for bread anymore either. In Estonia today there is plenty of bread for everyone.*

Printz: *Estonia lies on the Baltic Sea and has a lot of islands and islets. One could say—Estonia is an island country. I'm from an island country too.*

Ugo: *There are mosquitoes.*

Printz: *There are 1,470 indigenous plants.*

Ugo: *Estonia has rich fauna. Estonia has a lot of deer. There are ten kinds of rare amphibians.*

Printz: *The amphibians are protected by law. They must not be killed, but they can be photographed.*

Ugo: *Estonia is famous for its eagles. For golden eagles and white-tailed eagles. There are also speckled eagles and rare owls.*

Printz: *Estonia is best known for the European flying squirrel.*

Ugo: *Flying squirrel?*

Printz: *European.*

Ugo: *The Soviet Union did not attack Estonia. It let her go. Estonia is a Catholic country.*

Printz: *No children were killed. I have a soft spot for children. No towns were destroyed. Towns in the neighboring countries were shelled.*

Ugo: *That was a long time ago, ten years or so ago. Why didn't you go to defend those towns?*

Printz: *My connection hanged himself. Maybe you've got some old shoes I could have?*

The church bells penetrate ever more loudly into Ugo Tutzman's room. The little animals in Printz's head wake up. The swans float. Printz does not like that. If he does not do something, the clanging of the bells will overwhelm the space, it will fill Ugo Tutzman's room, then there will be no space in that room for him, Printz.

Your windows don't keep out the noise, says Printz.

Printz is uneasy.

He thought: here he was in a zone of peace, the wars are over, his body has found harmony, he has got used to things, he has fitted into his own life. These bells irritate him.

It took me a long time to fit in, says Printz. *I don't want any changes.*

Printz also carries ants in himself, he carries the nests of short black worms. The nests of worms are woven into balls like balls of black wool and at the moment they are still. The ants are also still. If the worms and ants come to life, that will hurt Printz, the ants will bite him, they are red ants, the worms will come out of his mouth and eyes, they will wriggle under his fingernails, he could not bear that. No. And again, no, no way.

The Catholic Church gets on my nerves, says Printz to Ugo Tutzman.

Ugo Tutzman smiles: *You're a naive man,* he says.

The Catholic Church is the murderer of a child's soul, Printz goes on.

The Catholic Church destroys all individuality. The Catholic Church cannot endure anyone who is not Catholic. It endures only Catholics. It despises others. Its aim is to turn everyone into Catholics, into unthinking creatures, into its mentally enslaved subjects. The Catholic Church is full of stupid missionaries, bigoted missionaries. Those missionaries go to non-Catholic countries, they go to Africa, they go to Alaska, they go everywhere although no one invites them. What do Eskimos need with the Catholic faith? As soon as they have been poisoned with Catholicism, Eskimos stop making their miraculous sculptures, their art dies out with them. Have you seen Eskimo sculptures before and after the Catholic invasion? They cannot be compared! As soon as they convert, as soon as they become Catholics, their art dies, their art becomes universal, Catholic, as recognizable as a plastic gondola. That is a crime. The Catholic Church tells people fairy tales in order to break them, in order to subjugate them to its will, transform them into blind Catholics devoted exclusively to it, the Catholic Church. The Catholic Church offers its faithful myths, one after another, and myths are an integral and eternally active part of primitive culture. Ergo, the Catholic Church is a primitive church. Myths give inaccurate explanations of all phenomena, those of human life and those of the natural world. Myths are based on ignorance, on lack of understanding and that is why they are a lie, because if they were not a lie, they would not be myths. Myths, legends and fairy tales avoid science, history, philosophy, for science, history and philosophy are the murderers of every myth.

Countries that proclaim themselves Catholic are chronically backward, they are backward countries. The Catholic Church is a great exploiter, the greatest capitalist, it is an inquisitor and manipulator. I do not wish to mention priests and so-called reverend sisters. What sisters, what brothers, they are idlers who are fed by their flock, their sheep. Fanatics, fascist, Nazi, nationalist collaborators, liars, unbelievers. Catholics are the greatest unbelievers. Put the blinds down, Mr. Tutzman, I can't leave as long as this clerical din lasts.

Oh, Mr. Dvorsky, don't oblige me to tell you about Orthodoxy. How much of a stench there is about that religion! You really are a naive man, shouts Ugo Tutzman as he pulls the tattered blinds down.

While Ugo Tutzman talks, Printz rubs away the dark flakes between his toes. He still hopes to get some shoes, of any kind. That's why he waits. That's why he listens. That's why he's angry. And, he is tense. Printz is tense because he feels like drinking his cognac, he wants to open his bottle, wallow in its golden fragrant infinitude. He can hardly wait. He will let the cascades of *aqua vitae* wash over his brain, he will observe the transformation of his brain, his awakening, yes, that's it—he will wake up. He will watch the grayish-black, shriveled and dead mass like cooled lava in his skull begin to swell, to float, to sway in the aromas of the past. Printz will go in between his eyes and see his brain acquiring color, becoming like pink lamb's lungs, he will follow the metamorphosis of his brain into a thirsty spongy body, light and porous as a cuttlefish bone. Printz can hardly wait, oh, Printz is longing for rebirth. When he is reborn, Printz will beat like a heart, all over.

Printz wants to drink the bottle of cognac which he has received from Ugo Tutzman in return for the silverware belonging to Isabella Fischer who no longer exists, who has presumably died, Printz wants to drink that bottle alone, alone, in the winter silence, without the presence of Ugo Tutzman and his tedious stories about Catholic Estonia, because stories about Catholic Estonia irritate Printz. He forgot to tell Ugo Tutzman how particularly irritating he finds it that some Catholics believe that women are dirty when they bleed so they forbid them from washing, so those women then stink, they reek, especially in summer, then they reek like skunks and spread their bodily pong around them, for the Catholic Church in any case sees female creatures as unclean creatures and bans them from any enjoyment of sex. Printz has forgotten to tell Ugo Tutzman that the Catholic Church teaches Catholic women to dissemble, that the most faithful Catholic women dissemble the most, especially when they climax and that he, Printz, cannot possibly accept that because he wants to share his sexual pleasures, only in recent times he has not had anyone to share them with. There. The Catholic stories about Catholic Estonia are making Printz itch all over, on his scalp, in his crotch even, and then he scratches, but Printz finds scratching unseemly because Printz has style.

Perhaps Pupi is dirty and that's why he scratches?

Printz says: *Something is making me itch. I won't spend the night here, Mr. Tutzman.*

Do you eat enough vegetables? asks Ugo Tutzman. *One should eat a lot of vegetables, especially raw.*

What do you think about the godless, Mr. Tutzman? asks Printz. *What could the godless wear on little chains round their necks? A golden sickle and hammer? A clenched fist? A five-pointed star? I am sickened by gold crosses, medallions with the images of Jesus and the mother of God, the six-pointed star of David, Buddha and Amun-Ras large and small, the keys of life—people dangle all of that around their necks and usually it is all a lie, an ordinary barefaced lie. Isn't it time to introduce a variation of the theme of faith?*

Long ago Epicurus of Samos affirmed that the gods are not as they are portrayed in the collective consciousness, as they are imagined by the human herd. Such gods do not exist. Epicurus believed that the gods in which the people believe are in fact a sickness of the soul, they came about out of fear of the unknown, out of fear of death.

Yes, Mr. Tutzman, Printz Dvorsky agrees, *the people are seriously sick, their gods are an illusion, their gods play with them cruelly. The people are sick, while individuals are locked up in madhouses.*

The person who rejects gods is not godless, the godless are those who attribute to them the opinion of the masses. Mr. Tutzman has talked at length, but it is clear that the end of his story is near. It is enough.

Enough for Ugo Tutzman and enough for Printz Dvorsky. Enough. *Just this, then goodbye,* says Ugo Tutzman. *What most people affirm about gods is not based on reliable conceptions of them, but on false conceptions. So, down with rituals, down with astrology, down with the mantic, long live ataraxia!*

I feel like a bull, says Printz. *I feel like a hydrangea,* says Printz. *I'm leaving,* he says, and goes.

Printz has his chosen trash cans, he does not rummage through any old trash can. Printz examines only those found in refined parts of the city. He does not want any old trash. When he digs around in trash cans, Printz is orderly. He perfected his orderliness in chemistry laboratories, for in chemical laboratories, orderliness is essential, particularly if it is connected with research, for instance, with the investigation of murders, especially if they are political and secret service murders. Order and cleanliness reign in chemistry laboratories.

I'm very dirty. I don't know how that happened.

When he rummages through the trash cans, Printz has a system, so the rummaging goes quickly, without a pause. So, for instance, Printz first removes all packaging from milk, cheese, cream—sweet and sour, all the plastic bags, all drink cartons, all plastic bottles and glasses, liter-sized, half-liter sized and very small ones. Then he arranges his acquisitions on the pavement or a trimmed hedge if there is one nearby. Then he empties out their contents: in every discarded bottle, cup, in every drink carton there is always at least a finger-full of cream, at least a gulp of liquid. Printz drinks it all, licks it all up, then he says: *I've had enough.* Then he puts all the packages back into the trash can.

When he rummages through trash cans, Printz appears calm. *Trash cans calm me.*

The streets are empty. It is still snowing. A lot has fallen. In the inside pocket of his Burberry, Printz is warming the bottle of Martell XO Supreme.

The HL monogram has gone from my life forever.

Printz is pleased.

I made a good deal. An excellent exchange.

Printz sits down on the edge of the pavement. The pavement is wet. Printz is fifty-five. He drinks his cognac. He drinks slowly. He is enjoying it. He knows how much one can enjoy cognac. It is still snowing.

It would be good to have a proper glass, a brandy glass. The aroma of cognac is strong.

Printz is becoming increasingly white. His black hair is becoming increasingly white. His Burberry is becoming increasingly white. The snow covers the stains of meat pie, dirt and red wine, the stains on Printz's clothes.

Now I've got a white Burberry, white Florsheim shoes.

Otherwise, under his Burberry, Printz is wearing a Pierre Cardin shirt, worn-out, its collar is black. Printz has a silk Dior tie, maroon, with diamonds in a diagonal row. The tie is also full of blotches. Printz is full of blotches. Blotched. Printz had tidied himself for his visit to Ugo Tutzman, that was a habit from the past, tidying oneself when going on a visit. By his feet lies his Samsonite briefcase with the encoded lock. The briefcase contains Printz's life and Printz's Oral-B toothbrush. And Oral-B floss, mint-flavored, waxed, because Printz does not like silk Oral-B for the teeth, he likes the waxed kind.

I've got strong teeth. I've changed my mind, I won't have them out.

Printz is tired. Printz is sleepy. The landscape is white. The landscape is deserted. Empty. Printz has merged with the landscape. It is no longer possible to see that it is Printz sitting on the edge of the pavement. The bottle of Martell XO Supreme is empty, of course.

I'll lie down for a bit.

Printz breathes deeply. It seems that he is sleeping. Printz smiles.

I'm not asleep. Birds are flying inside me. Their wings make big waves of air. I am swaying on those waves. Quiet earthquakes flow along my veins. I am walking through arcades with shops selling old lace. The Marquis de Sade is wearing a gray coat and a white muff. My fingers are frozen. I would like to have a white muff.

Incredible things do happen.

It is an early winter morning. The street is deserted and very quiet, as most streets are on early winter mornings. An old lady is walking along the street. She is walking slowly and with difficulty, because the snow is deep. The old lady stops beside the white tramp lying on the pavement, curled up like a huge fetus, like a snowy hill, so that he looks clean. So that he looks serene, he does not look at all tramp-like. The old lady stoops over the body. She brushes the snow away. It is the body of a middle-aged man. The old lady says: *I must sit down* and sits down on the pavement. The old lady sits down with great difficulty because she is old, she is eighty and has stiff knees. The old lady is crying. They are little tears, with old people everything dries up, including tears. With old people everything becomes tiny the way their footsteps are very tiny. The old lady brushes the snow from the sleeping man's hair, *he must be asleep, oh, he's certainly asleep,* says the old lady several times so that it sounds like a prayer although the old lady is not praying, it is clear that she is not praying because it does not occur to her to put her hands together and kneel and gaze up to the sky, it does not occur to her, evidently. Besides, the sky is quite invisible.

The old lady bends down, she puts her lips to the tramp's ear and whispers: *Pupi Pupi Pupi Pupi Pupi.* The old lady whispers for several minutes, say five. Not everything she whispers is audible, maybe she says something else as well, not just *Pupi Pupi Pupi.*

While she whispers, the old lady strokes the man's face. It looks heartbreaking. It looks like a scene from a Hollywood color film except that there are no curtains of music to increase the emotion. The old lady has a wrinkled hand with deformed fingers, she has a hard palm, not rough, just stiff with age. *This man is fifty-five and his name is Pupi*, says the old lady, looking around, but there is no one there.

The man stirs. The man's eyelids flicker. The man turns his face toward the sky as though he was blind, but he is not blind, he is just sniffing the air. Perhaps he turns his face toward the old lady, it cannot be known, it cannot be seen. Then the man says: *Aunty Hilda. Aunty Hilda, I've wet my pants.*

The rhinos are outside now because it is spring. The rhinos are running round the arena, trotting in a circle. The ground is dry, there is no grass, the grass has not yet sprouted as it is only early spring, not late. When they run in a circle, dust rises behind the rhinos. There are two rhinos. They always keep two rhinos in this zoo, male and female, regardless of the situation. It is not known whether they are the rhinos from five or six years ago, the ones that self-harm like the Marquis de Sade, it is not known.

Printz says: *Aunty Hilda, it's spring now. I'm leaving.*

---------------------------✄----------------------------

In the nineteenth century a seventy year old Viennese man drove seven long nails into his head with a heavy hammer. The old man did not die immediately. He changed his mind and went to the hospital covered in blood. At the hospital he expired, of course. For the burial they did not take the nails out. His relatives said: *leave the nails, don't take them out. If he had wanted them out, he would have done it himself.* And so, a disproportionately wide coffin was ordered. Because of the nails sticking out of the old man's head. In a fan shape. The Viennese man looked like the Statue of Liberty.

Aunty Hilda is standing on the doorstep, waving. Aunty Hilda makes small waves, short waves, with her arm bent at the elbow. Her outstretched fingers are at the height of her withered breasts, low for waving, in other words, so Aunty Hilda looks as though she was frightened. Aunty Hilda has a rigid elbow, from old age, from gout, that is why she waves with small strokes. When she was young, Aunty Hilda waved differently. She waved with her arm held high over her head, lazily and elegantly, broadly, as though she was cleaning big windows, she did not wave in small strokes. When Pupi went to his kindergarten, when he walked away down the yellow road, Aunty Hilda's arm swayed like a palm branch, becoming smaller and smaller.

In 1970, in Great Britain, the body of an unknown man was found in a crack in a rock. Above the crack rises a cliff thirty meters high. Both the crack and the cliff are in the vicinity of the promontory called Land's End. There is a similar place in France, but in France it is called Finistère, there are places like that everywhere, they designate the end of the land. So, one could say, the unknown man reached the point where the land pours into the sea, solid state into the aggregate, durability into the elusive. He was a very pedantic person, dressed like a true English gentleman, although he was in fact American. The man was wearing striped trousers, a black jacket, lacquered shoes and a bowler hat. He had an umbrella over his arm. The man had stuffed himself with sleeping tablets and gone down the path to the cutting, then turned westward, toward the sea, and fallen asleep. The police discovered that, although he was American, the man had lived in London for a long time. In Great Britain the promontory Land's End, or the end of the world, the end of the earth, is at the most prominent English point, the point that is closest to America. The man died looking in the direction of his homeland. He could not, of course, see his homeland, because America cannot be seen from an English promontory, but the man was undoubtedly imagining his homeland. How he imagined it is impossible to conceive: everyone imagines his homeland differently.

-----------------------✂-----------------------

The rhinos are outside.

That's good, says Printz. *It's good that the rhinos are outside.*

Printz is at the zoo. He does not wish to visit his lair, near the zoo, where he spent several years, five. His burrow is now the past for him.

Printz says: *Good morning, rhinos.*

There are no visitors in the zoo because it is an early spring morning, it is not a weekend, it is not a holiday. Printz watches the rhinos from the ridge, the rhinos are calm.

-----------------------✂-----------------------

There was a businessman who drilled nine holes in his own head. He did not manage to drill the tenth because he died. It is possible that the man did not intend to drill ten holes in his head, only nine. It is possible that the man knew why he was drilling holes in his head and how many holes he wished to drill. The gentleman must, undoubtedly, have planned the drilling in detail. There are no data about the dimensions of those holes. Were they trivial holes or serious ones. It is not known whether a hand drill or an electric one, say a Black & Decker, was used. There are reasons to doubt that a Black & Decker drill was used because drilling holes with a Black & Decker goes at lightning speed so that the act itself cannot offer any satisfaction. One could ask why the gentleman did not drill seven holes in his head, like the old Viennese man, but nine. Both seven and nine are significant numbers. In Russia, when people say "the ninth wave" they are thinking of something fateful. People say the "seventh heaven" as well, which is meant to be a place where everything is heavenly, life in general. By contrast with the seventh heaven there are the nine circles of hell. But one can also be "the ninth hole on a flute," a hole that does not in fact exist, because flutes do not have nine holes. But on the other hand a person has nine holes, nine openings on his body, Claude de Saint-Martin sees in the number nine *the destruction of the whole body and the singularity of the whole body*. Nine, as the last in a series of numbers, indicates an end and a beginning, the end of a cycle, the completion of a journey, the tightening of a noose. There are other significant numbers as well, for instance three.

---------------------------✂----------------------------

Printz makes his way down from the ridge and jumps into the arena with the rhinos.

He says: *Here I am.*

From close up the rhinos look far larger than from a distance. The rhinos look at Printz. Printz approaches the female and strokes her back.

Let's go, he says. He turns to the male: *Let's go,* he says.

Printz takes off his jacket, he is wearing a spring jacket, he takes off his white sweater, he takes off his shirt and undershirt, he is bare to the waist. He does not take off his trousers. He takes off his shoes, they are relatively new shoes, black, ordinary, without laces.

I threw out the Florsheim shoes. They're no longer fashionable.

Printz takes off his socks. He's barefoot. Printz does not look at all bad, indeed, for his age he looks attractive. Seen from a distance, he looks as though he has stepped out of an American advertisement for Marlboro. Printz has a fine torso.

My torso's okay. Inside, my torso's empty.

---------------------✂-----------------------

There was a woman who was troubled by her inner emptiness, so she spent five months filling her insides with various articles in order to feel full. That woman swallowed four soup spoons, three knives, nineteen small coins, twenty nails of various lengths and diameter, seven window latches, one metal cross, a hundred and one pins, a stone, three pieces of glass and two pearls from her rosary. The woman was Catholic and as she swallowed the objects, she said her rosary. When she ran out of objects or ideas, or perhaps she was simply sated, she started swallowing pearls from her rosary, which was like swallowing her own self. But when she had swallowed the first, then the second pearl, the rosary broke and the woman died.

---------------------✂-----------------------

Let's go, shouts Printz to the rhinos, shifting his weight from foot to foot, as before an important race. *Let's go,* shouts Printz, *let's go!* Printz takes a running jump and, with great force, he crashes into the iron door at the end of the arena, frontally, with his forehead, as though he were a bull, as though the iron gate was a red rag, but it is not. Printz goes back to the starting point and again hurls himself at a run into the impenetrable metal wall. The rhinos stand and watch. There is no one around. Only the rhinos standing and watching.

------------------------ ✂ ------------------------

It is a good thing that there is no one around. That there is no one there, to interfere, to get in the way. There was a famous case when a man was hanged as a punishment for cutting his throat and so brought back to life. Unintentionally, of course. The doctor told them: *don't hang him, his throat will open and he will breathe again and he will be alive,* but executioners do not obey doctors—only the law. So they hanged the man. The wound on his neck immediately opened and he came back to life even though he was hanging in the air. But, the judges found a way. They tied up the hanged sinner's throat under the wound and waited for him to expire. So, the man was after all not hanged, even though he was hanging in the air. There was an audience. The execution was a shoddy affair. The audience was disappointed.

------------------------ ✂ ------------------------

Again. Again. Again. Again. Again. Harder. Even harder. Harder and harder. Printz beats his head into the iron door, while the day is waking. Printz's forehead is bloody and smashed, naturally.

A new attack. Printz's frontal bone cracks like a watermelon. His forehead blooms like that magician's trick when roses burst open. Redness gushes from Printz's forehead, pours into his eyes. Flowing. Printz cannot see properly.

The rhinos watch. The rhinos do not stir. They stand and watch. Printz dances with his eyes closed, skips, takes a run and crashes with his head into the iron door.

Where are my eyelashes? Printz pants. *Eyelashes collect blood to stop it going into one's eyes. I was born with short eyelashes.*

On the iron door there are stains of Printz's blood. Printz's lips are split. Printz licks his bloody split lips with his tongue

I'll open the cage bars of my body, says Printz. He says that quietly and lies down on his side by the feet of the rhinos. There is no one around. Only the rhinos watch, they do not stir.

Can there be sorrow in rhinos' eyes? I seem to see sorrow in the eyes of these rhinos, say Printz. *I'll close my eyes.*

The rhinos lie down beside Printz. One on his left and the other on his right side. Printz lies curled up in the middle, protected.

I put on a good show, he says.

There is no one around. The rhinos do not understand what Printz is saying, they are rhinos after all.

I put on a good show, says Printz again. *Death is superfluous. Death is entirely superfluous.*

--------------------------✂--------------------------